MY FIRST STORY 2018

Welcome!

Dear Reader,

Welcome to a world of imagination!

My First Story was designed for Key Stage 1 children as an introduction to creative writing and to promote an enjoyment of reading and writing from an early age.

The simple, fun storyboards give even the youngest and most reluctant writers the chance to become interested in literacy by giving them a framework within which to shape their ideas. Pupils could also choose to write without the storyboards, allowing older children to let their creativity flow as much as possible, encouraging the use of imagination and descriptive language.

We believe that seeing their work in print will inspire a love of reading and writing and give these young writers the confidence to develop their skills in the future.

There is nothing like the imagination of children, and this is reflected in the creativity and individuality of the stories in this anthology. I hope you'll enjoy reading their first stories as much as we have.

Jenni Harrison
Editorial Manager

Imagine...

Each child could choose one of five storyboards, using the pictures and their imagination to create an exciting tale. You can view the storyboards at the end of this book.

There was also the option to create their own story using a blank template.

AMAZING ADVENTURES
CONTENTS

Tyarna-Leigh Davies (6) 60

Prendergast Community Primary School, Prendergast

Alexis Hamilton-Simmons (7)	61
Holly Helga Jane Thomas (6)	62
Connor Halsall (6)	64
Kenuli Himadya Wickramaarchchi (6)	65
Megan Roos Conings (6)	66
Charlotte Ella Isaac (6)	67
Jacob Smith (6)	68
Lucas Cameron Hull (7)	69
Oliver Harri Lowe (7)	70
Sam Warneford (6)	71
Mollie Mathias (6)	72
Lucas Tate (6)	73
Josh Oxley (6)	74
Zac Morris (6)	75
Tomos William Blyth (5)	76
Charlie Dunthorne (6)	77
Caitlin Jackson (7)	78
Reuben Thomas (6)	79
Callum Ceri Davies (6)	80

Quainton CE Primary School, Quainton

Millie Webster (6)	81
Scarlett Ashton (6)	82
Harriet Aplin (6)	83
Harry William Espiner (6)	84
Jake Kehoe (6)	85
Harley Sayell (6)	86
Dilan Marudamuthu (6)	87
Ava Patricia Read (6)	88
Alice Carlisle (6)	89

Rogerstone Primary School, Rogerstone

Lucas Thompson (7)	90
Alfie Downs (6)	91
Lauren	92
Emily Faulds (6)	93

William Jude Woodley (6)	94
Dewi Munn (6)	95
Olivia (7)	96
Pietro Christopher Kaye (6)	97
Ffion Rose Newman (6)	98
Lydia Porter (6)	99
Brooke Barnes (7)	100
Katy Cooper (6)	101
Dylan Hugh Matthews (6)	102
Benjamin Jacob Jones (6)	103
Theo Austin Phillips (6)	104
Rylie-Faye Harry-Young (6)	105
Ella Manning (6)	106
Isla Mae Fox-Smith (6)	107
Grace Davis (6)	108
Emilia Wendy Casagrande (6)	109
Max Chambers (5)	110
Corey Jai Morris (6)	111
Zachary Slade	112
Poppy Marie Davies (6)	113
Mackenzie Stone	114
Shouvik Sengupta (6)	115
Harvey Tayor (6)	116
Gracie Meyrick	117
Freya Williams (6)	118
Hazel May Read (5)	119
Oliver Bowen (6)	120
Freddie Hayes (6)	121
Maia-Tlws Blackler	122

Sekolah Darma Bangsa School, Kedaton

Delisha Saabira Yasni	123

Sound Primary School, Lerwick

Thomas Steven Burden (6)	124
Connor Burgess (6)	125
Natalia Kerr Leggate (5)	126
Nina Hughson (5)	127
Ella-Mae Gair (5)	128
Jacob Henderson (5)	129
Daniel Anderson (6)	130
Lowrie Nicol (6)	131

Lewie Johnston (5) 132
Zena Roseanne Wiseman (6) 133
Freya Byrne (5) 134
Corren Williamson (5) 135
Cole Kay (5) 136
Magnus Leask (6) 137
Amie Coleman (6) 138
Theo Spence (6) 139
Lily-May McLean (5) 140
Adam Spence (6) 141
Luca Thomason (6) 142
Leila Hall (6) 143
Darcey Henry (5) 144
Leon Priestley (5) 145
Charlie More (5) 146
Oarryn Mann (5) 147
Natas Engum (5) 148
Nathan Ross (5) 149
Alfie Tozer (5) 150
Alec Arthur (6) 151
Daniel Henry (6) 152
Nebble March (5) 153
Bella Smith (5) 154

St Mary's Primary School, Portaferry

Lily Jennifer Trainor (7) 155
Cahlie Boyd (7) 156
Eva-Marie Curran (7) 157
Francis Keating (7) 158
Ellie McGrattan (7) 159
Caitlin Ritchie (7) 160
Jude Coleman (7) 161
Joel McKenna (7) 162
Scarlett Trainor (7) 163
Caitlin Hall (7) 164
Evan Morgan (7) 165
Lily-May Elizabeth Marshall (7) 166
Kenzie McCluskey (7) 167

St Patrick's Primary School, Aughagallon

Rose Tallon (7) 168
Katrina Brankin (7) 169
Ronan Hughes (7) 170
Anna Corey (7) 171
Eva Anna-Marie Lavery (6) 172
Jay Mulholland (7) 173
Charlie Nelson (7) 174

Stanwix Primary School, Carlisle

George Edward Heaps (5) 175
Sophia Willow Rawlings-Brown (5) 176
Mathilde Zayer (5) 177
Annabel Fraser (5) 178
Arman Kalam (4) 179
Harriet Ryding (5) 180
Austin Barry (4) 181
Thomas Van Lierop (4) 182

Stepaside CP School, Kilgetty

Angharad Bowen (6) 183
Jacqueline Dunfee (7) 184
Liam Lee 185
Lisa Stevens (6) 186
Connor James Jones (7) 187

Ysgol Y Graig, Lon Talwrn

Ella Wyn Bird (7) 188
Ella Wyn Jones (6) 189
Adam Pumfrey (7) 190
Bobby Parry (7) 191
Lowri Evans (7) 192
Gruffudd Huw Redvers Jones (7) 193
Iolo Williams (6) 194
Lexi Parry (7) 195
Ffion Haf Griffith (7) 196
Maya Golaski (7) 197
Cadi Lois Parry (7) 198
Owain Rhys Jones (6) 199
George Henry Junior Takyi (7) 200

The Stories

Monster House

One spooky, creepy night, there lived a vampire called Sam. His parents were ghosts, they were scary. It was Halloween so every spooky kid went trick or treating. Sam saw his creepy brother and sister's house. His sister said, "Come on Sam, you're going to be late for the party!"

Sam thought, *what's going on?*

Then Sam's friend, Zach, came and said, "Are you going to the party? Yesterday, your sister texted everyone saying there's a party at your house." When Sam got to his house, he started to dance. There was jazzy music. They were playing hide-and-seek and Sam said, "Boo!" Sam and his friends had a disco with lots of sweets.

"See you later, Sam," they said when it was time to go home.

Jacob Thorne

Buzzy Bee Land

It was a warm, sunny afternoon in the month of June. Miss Kelly, our teacher, took our class outside for a little story and play. While we were listening to the story, we heard a 'buzzzzz' and saw a bee creeping along on the playground. Its wings were soaking, it was really tired and it couldn't fly at all. Miss Kelly told the class that bees are God's angels. They shouldn't be allowed to die. We ran inside to get some sugary water to feed the bee. Miss Kelly fed the bee and then we all went inside so the bee could rest. We called her Buzzy Bee.

At lunchtime, we were all shocked to see that Buzzy Bee was dead. We laid the bee on the sand and covered it with grass and summer flowers. I wondered where the bee would go now. I secretly wished I knew.

That night, I heard a buzzing sound in my ear. It was Buzzy Bee! "How did you get here?" I asked. Buzzy Bee said, "I have come from Buzzy Bee Land. Would you like to come along with me? The golden angels of Buzzy Bee Land would like to see you all because you were all so kind and nice to me." Buzzy Bee took me on her back and buzzed away to Buzzy Bee Land.

It was a land of golden light ruled by Queen Bee and her little angel bees. There was a river of honey flowing along. There were flowers made of sugary lollipops. Ice cream seeds sprouted into delicious ice cream cones. The bee houses were made of honeycomb and candyfloss. It was so soo nice, I couldn't believe my eyes. I could eat as much ice cream and candyfloss and lollipops as I wished, Queen Bee told me. Yummy! It was so delicious. I went into the bee houses on Buzzy Bee's back and we flew and flew and flew so happily all over golden Buzzy Land.

A golden angel bee suddenly appeared and told me that it was time to go back. Buzzy Bee took me back home. Buzzy Bee said she loved me and would miss me a lot.

When I woke up that morning, I saw everything was back to normal. Where was Buzzy Bee, the angels and fairies? Mummy told me that Miss Kelly and the class were the angels... When you are kind and nice you are angels after all.

Niharika Menon (5)

The Tournament

Once, there was a sabre-toothed tiger who was very fierce and wanted to win the tournament that took place every four years.

"To win, I must be strong," roared the sabretooth. So he went out of his brown, wooden den to the dark black forest because he wanted to find a large animal to test his strength on.

However, he found a mammoth in front of a tall brown tree. He said, "Can you challenge me?"

The large mammoth said, "Yes." So they fought. The sabretooth used teeth rip but the mammoth dodged it very quickly. The sabretooth thought extremely quick about the mammoth's next move, and *ping!* He saw his next move in his head. It was tusk swipe. So he used turbo scratch and the huge mammoth fell to the ground straight away. The sabretooth knocked the furious beast out. The mammoth was really shocked.

He said, "Wow! You must have trained well. Are you going to the tournament?"

"Yes!"

"I will tell you where to find the location." So the mammoth gave a map to him. "Good luck," said the friendly mammoth.

"Bye," replied the sabretooth.

After that, the sabretooth returned to his hut and studied the brown map. He got out his amazing microscope so he would know where to go. Then he saw the village and at the end of the village was the tournament.

Himat Singh Bering (7)

Lily's Magical Story

... a big, golden castle, they were inside. The castle had a garden. Soon, they met a fairy called Emma Flower. "I'm a special fairy who can grant wishes." Emma asked for a house made of candy. All of a sudden, an ugly troll appeared inside. The troll was messy and he was short. The troll lived in a lovely house and it was made out of candy. It looked brilliant, it had a marshmallow chimney and its roof was made from icing. Inside there was gingerbread and the kitchen was made out of marshmallows and there were balloons and presents. They had a great party then went home.

Lily Stewart (9)

Grace's Magical Story

... a magical, fairy tale castle, Emma and Ben were so happy to see what was in there! When they went in, they saw a beautiful fairy sitting on a mushroom. She was very pretty. Her name was Snowfrost. They saw a smelly troll! It was very ugly. There was something sitting over on the hill so they walked up to see what was there, it was a dog. The dog started to nibble on the candy cane. The troll and Snowfrost came to the party. They had lots of fun. Soon, they went out of the magical tree and they brought some cake with them. They had a great time!

Grace Stewart (9)

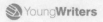
Enchanted Land

Once upon a time, there was a fairy's house by a rainbow. It was lovely, so cute, so beautiful and amazing! A unicorn lived there called Emily.
Once, there was a dragon called Borris. He tried to burn down the house but he couldn't. Emily was scared and nervous. The unicorn said hello to the dragon and they shook hands. They were friends. The dragon flew away and Emily was sad and tried to bring him back but it was dark, so the unicorn set off back home. They all lived happily ever after.

Noa Ariane Din

Very Scary Vampire And Samby

One day, there was a very scary vampire called Trick or Treat. He knocked on a door but no one answered so he went to a haunted house and some people were walking. He saw Samby, he just kept walking. "Boo! Are you coming to my Halloween party?"
"Let's play hide-and-seek!" Then they had a party.

Seantai Nugent

The Runaway Babies!

Once upon a time, there were three babies called Holly, Silky and Lilly. It was night-time, they had been planning to escape so they got out of bed and went downstairs, then they went to the door and pushed it but it was locked...

They went back upstairs and into their room, they remembered their parents had opened the window and forgot to shut it. So they headed to the window and jumped out. They landed in different positions.

The alarm went off, the babies heard it, they ran onto the street and called a taxi. The taxi went to the president's house. The babies went in to see the president, he was a man with a big moustache and he was extremely fat. The babies started to attack! As soon as they got the president laying down, they started bouncing on his belly like on a trampoline! Then they locked him in the cupboard and they all became presidents.

One day they opened the cupboard, the old president was dead. "Oh well," said Holly.

"He was never very nice," said Lilly.

"His knickers stink!" said Silky, throwing a pair of pants in the washing basket. Then they locked the cupboard again.

The babies were bored now, they didn't have anything to do. So they decided to play in the garden, in-between the bushes. There was something that hadn't been there before. It was a portal! The babies went in, the portal whooshed round and round... Suddenly, they came out in a weird land. Holly licked a tree cos she always does that. "Caramel!" she yelled. "Try it!" Everyone tried it.

"Caramel!" yelled Lilly. "It's scrumptious!"

Silky licked the tree. "Caramel!"

Then they went looking for other stuff to eat, they could eat anything they liked.

They went walking through the street eating everything they wanted. Silky even managed to get a doorknob. Suddenly, a big wind blew and the land started to spin round and round... The babies ran round and round, shouting, "What's happening?" They spotted a hole and went down, there was a ladder. They climbed down and realised they were at a tree. There was a yellow door. The babies went through, there was a note that said: 'I have moved out so you can move in'. The person had left some great stuff.

In no time the babies moved in and made friends with those who also lived in the tree. They also discovered that different lands were at the top of the tree. The babies visited the lands that were all different.

Siri Taylor (6), Libby Cole & Hannah Daisy Farquharson

Craiglockhart Primary School, Edinburgh

The Vegetable Invasion

Once, there was a girl called Viola and another girl called Shoana. They were BFFs but one day, there was a noise like a car that had started an engine. They went over to it and the noise got louder and louder. Then out of a spaceship came some vegetables and a wizard that turned all the vegetables into real, alive vegetables! The wizard said, "My army of vegetables, we will chase the humans out of Earth and we will make the vegetables alive!"

"Shoana, this is bad, isn't it?" said Viola.

Shoana said, "Yes, let's tell the news people." So they ran and ran and they finally got the news people but no one believed them so they climbed on the spaceship, then they thought.

"Wait a minute," said Viola, "they are all vegetables. We can put them in a pan and cook them, then sell them because they're all in here!"

"So let's get started!" said Shoana. So they did it and they took the wizard's wand and saved the future!

Cady Man-Smith (7)

Craiglockhart Primary School, Edinburgh

Pugerfly And Co

One day, Pugerfly, Faicat and Guineacorn went exploring in Cotton Candy Forest. They ran so far that they found a huge tree house in the middle of the forest. They heard loud laughter coming from inside. Pugerfly said, "Why don't we look inside?" So they looked inside and saw Pandacorn, Unikitty, Puppycorn and Unicorn Poop.

The second they walked in, Unicorn Poop said, "Hey guys!"

Pandacorn, Unikitty and Puppycorn all said, "Oh no, run!" So they all ran.

Pandacorn said, "Quick, into my house!" So they went to Pandacorn's house and hid and hoped that Unicorn Poop wouldn't find them.

After a while, Pugerfly said, "Why are we hiding?"

Pandacorn said, "Unicorn Poop is the most annoying thing in the world!"

"That's why she's so good at defeating baddies, she's so annoying, they stay away," said Puppycorn.

"I don't think she's coming," said Faicat, so they got out of their places and played snap until the day was over.

The next day, they went back to Cotton Candy Forest, to the tree house and went to pick kiwicorns from the trees until Centipig and Fasp came along and tried to start a war. They spent all day fighting with Centipig and Fasp until Draga came and stopped the war. Centipig and Fasp went away, then Unicorn Poop said, "Hey guys!"

Annie Pantopoulou (7)
Craiglockhart Primary School, Edinburgh

Mrs Goo-Goo The Baby Teacher

Mrs Goo-Goo, the baby teacher, had a very important lesson for her class. It was how to pick your boogers and eat them! The class was very excited until they heard it included boogers. When it was time to do it, the baby teacher did a very long poo so she missed the lesson, they had to cope with the baby teacher crying for a year! Suddenly, there was a unicorn in the classroom. The baby teacher started saying, "Goo, goo!" The children picked her up and put her on the unicorn's back. The unicorn started galloping, the baby teacher was having fun. Suddenly, the unicorn stopped and more unicorns appeared and a dragon.

"Wow!" The dragon fought with the unicorns but the unicorns had more powers so they defeated the dragon.

The children were so noisy that more dragons came but the unicorns had no powers left and got defeated.

The dragons ruled the world forever.

Kate Marshall (7)
Craiglockhart Primary School, Edinburgh

Armelle's Under The Sea Story

Once upon a time, there was a little cottage beside a big wood. On the other side of the woods, there was a big, wide sea. In the big, wide sea, there was a big bunch of coral. There were little holes in the coral, there were little fishes. One little fish had pink and blue polka dots. One of the fishes had white and blue polka dots, he was the king fish. The king fish had a big, golden crown that he found at the bottom of the sea.

Back in the cottage, the little girl was sad but her family had a surprise for her. They were going to the beach!

Armelle Le Buhan (6)
Craiglockhart Primary School, Edinburgh

Dragons Rule!

Once upon a time, there was a lovely castle with lovely people living there but one person was not nice and she was very spoilt. She wanted to rule the land. She wanted to rule the country. She wanted to rule the world!

One day, a dragon came. The princess was hiding in every place she could find but the dragon spotted her. He chased her and chased her and chased her! He was still chasing her until the prince came to save her! The guards said, "Do you want me to get her?"

The queen said, "You know what? No!"

Ayla Kocak Rye (7)
Craiglockhart Primary School, Edinburgh

The Amazing Trip To The Moon

Once upon a time, there was a dog called Georgie. She was going to space with me and my sister, Marlie, in a rocket.

When we arrived, we met an alien called Scout. She was very friendly. Scout had four eyes, she was so cool! We jumped so high that we went back to the dinosaur times! A stegosaurus nearly ate us but it didn't. We then saw a time machine so we went in and travelled back to 2018.

Erin (7) & Marlie Eva Rankin
Craiglockhart Primary School, Edinburgh

Pikachu And Chuchu Go To Space

Pikachu and Chuchu went to space. They found a Pokémon, then they found another live Pokémon. Wait, no it wasn't, it was a dead Bellsprout! Aliens had killed him. They were horrified. So they killed the aliens with their powers, then Slenderman came. John Cena then came up, he was an alien with a green tummy. He beat Slenderman but then John Cena died.

Oskar McIntosh (7)
Craiglockhart Primary School, Edinburgh

William's Dinosaur Story

In 1982, a man called Limpe Setolp invented a time machine called Antdesetablast. Limpe Setolp tested the time machine and it worked! It went back 65,000 years to the dinosaur times! When he got through, he saw a T-rex. He only had five minutes before the time machine went back but it was too late, the time machine went!
Nine years later, he got eaten by a T-rex.

William Heeps (8)

Craiglockhart Primary School, Edinburgh

The Dragon, The Unicorn And The Castle

Once, there was a castle in a sunny, hot land where there was always a rainbow of bright colours and the plants grew beautifully and smelt great.

One day, a terrifying dragon came to the castle. He wanted to burn the castle down. Everyone was scared! The dragon flew towards the castle, everyone ran to the tree. Then the dragon burnt down the castle but everyone was safe. The nasty dragon burnt the whole castle down. The king and queen that lived there were heartbroken! Then, a very special unicorn came, she had a twisty horn and clear, bright blue eyes. She told the dragon how mean he'd been and fixed a deal that he'd never do it again. The dragon flew back to where he came from and the unicorn put the fire out and made sure everyone was safe. They were safe.

"But what about the castle?" the king and queen asked.

The unicorn turned around three times and flashed her eyes of blue and made a new home for the king and queen.

"Thank you," said the king and queen.
The unicorn and the king and queen lived happily
ever after.

Emily Bruce (7)

Goodly Dale Primary School, Windermere

Under The Sea

Once, there was a boat with nobody in it. It was floating on the surface of the sea. It started to get stormy, the boat started to sink. The sea creatures saw the shade from the boat above. They heard the boat breaking. They swam as fast as they could.

A shark heard the boat breaking and went to see what was happening. All the fish swam to help the little fish get out from the big pile of wood. The mermaid and the shark heard from the sea king that they had released the little fish from the pile of wood. They all cheered. The sea king had a party with everyone. They were all tired. Suddenly, the sea king said, "We will not stop this party!" They all went up to the surface of the sea and waved to the humans. "We're having a party, come and join us. Please, come!"

Erica Lindsay Rosa Beattie (7)
Goodly Dale Primary School, Windermere

The Dragon And The Unicorn Story

Once upon a time, there was a lovely castle. There was a tree next to the castle.

One day, a dragon came. He said, "Hello, is anyone in?" Nobody answered. He asked again and again and again, nobody answered. Because nobody answered, he blew out his fierce fire and the castle burnt down into little pieces! Then a unicorn came to defeat the dragon.

"Hey!" shouted the unicorn.

The dragon shouted back, "What?"

"Why is that castle on fire?" asked the unicorn.

"Hmm, I don't know," alarmed the dragon, then he flew away. The unicorn trotted to a cottage, it was dark so the unicorn went to bed.

Amelia Gooden (7)
Goodly Dale Primary School, Windermere

Seryn's Magical Story

Once upon a time, there was a beautiful unicorn and her name was Beauty, Beauty had a friend. Beauty's friend was a princess. The unicorn and the princess were playing a game when a dragon appeared and blew down the castle. Everybody went to hide, the dragon was left alone. The dragon didn't mean to burn down the castle! But then, the unicorn came out of her hiding place and she said, "Why are you here?"
The dragon said, "I want a friend."
The unicorn said, "I will be your friend."
"You're the best," said the dragon. And from them on, no more dragons went back to the castle.

Seryn Daisy Lowe (7)
Goodly Dale Primary School, Windermere

Luke's Dinosaur Story

Long, long ago, a little boy found a time machine. He went inside, then he saw a lever that he pulled. *Bam!* He noticed he was in the dinosaur time. He saw a stegosaurus and a brachiosaurus and a volcano, then he saw a T-rex. He looked fierce and he had sharp teeth. He saw the boy and he ran into the jungle. It was terrifying! The boy took the eggs from the nest and jumped out of the tree. The mum saw the boy had the eggs. The mum dived and grabbed the eggs. They started to hatch. Then the pterodactyl said, "You can have them."
The boy saw the time machine and whizzed back home. He lived happily ever after.

Luke Enright-Price (6)
Goodly Dale Primary School, Windermere

The Unicorn And The Dragon

Once upon a time, there was a girl called Lily. She went on a walk to the forest and she went so deep in the forest, Lily saw a castle. There was a dragon, he was called Tom. He was a guard but he was a mean dragon so Lily said, "Please can I come in?" But Tom didn't let her in. Tom blew fire! A unicorn came and the unicorn had a forcefield so Lily was safe.

The unicorn said, "Get away!" But the dragon didn't go away so Lily scared Tom away. The dragon flew away and he was never seen again.

It was Lily's dinner time so Lily said, "Can I ride you back home?"

Katie Milligan (7)
Goodly Dale Primary School, Windermere

Under The Sea

Once upon a time, there was a random boat. It was a cloudy day and the boat was very old. There was a shark and it bit a hole in the boat! Under the sea, there were happy creatures but the seaweed was swooshy because of the big bad shark. The big bad shark scared all the sea creatures away. Suddenly, the mermaid came and she whacked her tail and scared the shark away. Then the mermaid king, the mermaid and all the sea creatures had a party to celebrate. Finally, the mermaid and the mermaid king waved goodbye to the magical boat.

Evie Lofthouse (7)
Goodly Dale Primary School, Windermere

Afra's Magical Story

Once upon a time, there was a unicorn and she lived with a little girl called Anna. She was extraordinary, interested in maths and she did everybody favours by hanging up the washing. Then, a terrifying dragon came and tore down the washing and started breathing out fire onto the castle! Anna was shocked. The unicorn said to the dragon, "Stop it, you're doing the wrong thing! Go away!" Suddenly, the dragon gave a loud shriek and flew away. The unicorn was happy and flew away.

Afra Lily Lowe (7)
Goodly Dale Primary School, Windermere

Josh's Dinosaur Story

Once upon a time, there was a little boy called James. He bought a time machine. He went in the time machine and came out in the dinosaur time. James spotted a T-rex and ran away. The T-rex chased James through the scary jungle. Suddenly, James fell over a nest of T-rex eggs. He took one. A pterodactyl chased James so he ran back and put the T-rex's egg back in the nest. Then James ran back to the time machine and went back home. He ran to his mum and went back inside his house.

Josh Harvey (7)
Goodly Dale Primary School, Windermere

A Magical Unicorn

One day, there was a castle and a unicorn came to the castle, it was amazing! Then a dragon came but it just wanted a friend. "You can be my friend," said the princess. But then a mean dragon came and the dragon blew fire. The princess said, "Stop!" The unicorn came and she hurt the dragon. She scared the dragon away. "Hooray!" said the princess. "Yay! Yay! Yay!" The unicorn went around the house, the castle was around the house.

Maya Stratula (7)
Goodly Dale Primary School, Windermere

Samuel's Dinosaur Story

One day, Sam looked in his garden. He found a time machine so he travelled back to the time of dinosaurs. The landscape was beautiful, dinosaurs were everywhere that he looked! Suddenly, a T-rex jumped out of the bush. It wasn't friendly and it chased Sam all the way to an erupting volcano. He ran the opposite way but the T-rex wasn't chasing Sam, he was running after his eggs to save them from getting cold and the babies not hatching. He saved all of them.

Samuel Maxim Grman (6)
Goodly Dale Primary School, Windermere

Oscar's Under The Sea Story

Once upon a time, there was a fish called Kevin and he was swimming extremely quickly because there was a shark coming to get him! The shark was trying to make friends, even though he looked fierce, he was lonely. A beautiful mermaid waved at the shark to make friends, then a crab, a seahorse and some dancing mermaids invited the shark to a party. Kevin the fish became friends with the shark. They played together with mermaids forever.

Oscar (6)
Goodly Dale Primary School, Windermere

The Magical Sea

In the sea, there was a happy mermaid and on the surface, there was a boat near the shore. It found an island. A crab was looking for a pearl but the crab caught something out of the corner of his eye. It was a shark, a huge shark! It was going to eat the fish but then the mermaid scared the shark away and the shark was never seen again. The mermaids had a celebration because the shark was gone. The mermaids said goodbye to the boat.

Phea Niamh Tyson (7)
Goodly Dale Primary School, Windermere

George's Dinosaur Story

Long, long ago, Ronan saw a time machine. He travelled back in time to the creepy land of dinosaurs. A T-rex jumped out of the jungle. The T-rex was about to grab the eggs but Ronan scared him away. The eggs belonged to a pterodactyl. The pterodactyl was mad at Ronan because he was friends with the T-rex and the T-rex was trying to protect the eggs. Ronan jumped back onto the time machine and travelled back to the land of humans.

George Matthew Cousins (7)
Goodly Dale Primary School, Windermere

Noah's Dinosaur Story

Long, long ago, Vonet made a time machine. He travelled back in time to the Jurassic period. A mean T-rex crept quietly through the jungle. He was as hungry as a tiger! He had not eaten for months. The T-rex went to eat the eggs. Vonet jumped out and saved three eggs. The T-rex passed a pterodactyl while it was running away. Vonet travelled back to human time. He came back home and ran as fast as he could.

Noah (6)
Goodly Dale Primary School, Windermere

Kaitlin's Magical Story

Once upon a time, there was a fairy princess. She found a magic unicorn and played with it. It was dinner time and a dragon hid behind the castle. The scary dragon burnt the castle down with red-hot fire. It then chased the magical unicorn. The unicorn used some magic to make the dragon disappear. The dragon got smaller and smaller until you couldn't see it anymore. The unicorn went back home safely.

Kaitlin Demaine (6)
Goodly Dale Primary School, Windermere

My New Sea Friend

One scorching afternoon, I went on my boat into the Pacific Ocean and left my boat abandoned and went scuba diving. At first, I saw a crab dancing and waving his claws at me. He showed me a clownfish, a zebrafish and a starfish. They were looking for food. Then we saw a shark, it was going to eat us! It was really scary with the sharpest teeth ever. Even the hermit crab hid in his shell. Suddenly, a beautiful mermaid appeared with her dad. He scared the shark away, then me and the mermaid became friends, her name was Lilly. The shark ran away as fast as lightning. The king and his daughter were over the moon!

Me, the crab, Lilly, and the king were dancing. The seahorse thanked the king. We said goodbye but agreed I would go to the middle of the sea to play with Lilly every day.

Andi-May Watson (8)
Kirkshaws Primary School, Coatbridge

My Sea Adventure

On a scorching day, I went scuba diving in the Indian Ocean. I was looking for cool stuff. At first, I saw a school of fish in the background, they were looking for food. A busy crab came by and it seemed it was waving its claws. Suddenly, a great white shark appeared, its teeth were as sharp as the point of a knife. It was hunting for food. A lovely mermaid appeared beside the great white shark. It was about to swallow the mermaid but her dad saved her. The shark went away as fast as he could.

Neptune and the mermaid were safe, the crab waved its claws and danced. The seahorse said, "Thank you very much!" I was waiting for them to go away so I could sail away. They waved goodbye.

Nico McKirkle (7)
Kirkshaws Primary School, Coatbridge

Under The Sea

Me and Macie hired a rowing boat and went into the middle of the sea, then we jumped off. We had scuba diving suits on, we were excited. When we'd dived in, we saw a little crab in the ocean. The crab was snapping away. After, we saw a smiley shark with his big, sharp teeth and a hermit crab hiding in a shell. Then, Neptune came and gave the shark a fright and it swam away! We were so happy. Then we had a party with a mermaid and King Neptune. We danced all around the sea. The crab was clicking his claws. Then we had to go home. We said bye and rowed home. We would always remember the fun time we had under the sea.

Amy Adam
Kirkshaws Primary School, Coatbridge

Under The Sea

Me and my friend jumped off the rowing boat to explore under the sea with our wetsuits and scuba masks. We went deep and met a dancing crab snapping his claws. We swam on and met a smiling shark with sharp, pointy teeth and a hermit crab hiding in its shell. We were very scared, then we saw a mermaid and her dad, Neptune. The shark was scared because he was the king of the sea. I felt relieved. We had a dance battle. Unfortunately, the mermaid won. They kindly took us back to the boat and said goodbye. We felt sad our time under the sea was over for this year.

Corey Dawson McFarlane
Kirkshaws Primary School, Coatbridge

Under The Sea

Stephen and I were riding a rowing boat, then we jumped into the sea. With our scuba stuff, we went deep down into the sea and saw a crab dancing. We swam along and saw a smiley shark with sharp teeth. There was a hermit crab hiding from the shark in a shell. Then a mermaid and her dad came and scared the shark off. The shark never came back again. Then we had a party because they won against the shark and we were happy. They said goodbye to us because it was home time.

Christopher Dougan (6)
Kirkshaws Primary School, Coatbridge

The Unicorn Castle

A long time ago, there was a blue and pink castle. Everyone was happy, it was always sunny. In the castle, there lived a pink unicorn.

One day, a red dragon came. The dragon wanted to destroy the castle! The dragon tried to blow it down but he couldn't. He tried his best but he still couldn't. It was because he didn't have that much fire in his mouth. The dragon saw the unicorn and the unicorn said, "Why do you want to blow down the castle?"

The dragon said, "I'm not telling you." So the unicorn kicked the dragon, its leg hurt from the unicorn's powerful kick. The unicorn was kind so it gave the dragon a wish. The dragon wished for a house.

The unicorn said, "Only if you're kind to everyone!"

Lauren Frazer (7)
Northside Primary School, Northside

Sniffy And The Dangerous Dragon

Many years ago, there was a royal castle and in it, there was a unicorn called Sniffy and she was cleaning. Suddenly, a fierce dragon called Rocky was at the window. Rocky scratched his talons down the castle walls with a screeching sound. Rocky tried to burn the castle down but it didn't work. Sniffy was scared but she calmed down. Rocky went inside the castle and Sniffy appeared, then they had a fight and Rocky flew away crying. Sniffy was relieved but still a bit frantic. Sniffy lived happily ever after.

Tai O'Leary (7)
Northside Primary School, Northside

The Little Castle

Once upon a time, there was a pretty, little castle. There was a princess inside. Her name was Princess Peach.

The next day, a dragon came and tried to burn the castle down. The dragon attacked the castle with hot, orange fire. It didn't work. The castle was too strong. The unicorn came and scared the dragon away and poked him with her horn. The dragon flew away and the unicorn felt happy.

Finally, the unicorn went home. She was tired but content.

Mason Donoghue (6)
Northside Primary School, Northside

The Unicorn And The Dragon

One day, in a faraway land, there was a beautiful, pink castle.

The next day, a dragon came and tried to burn it down!

Hours later, the dragon tried to burn it down again.

The next day, the unicorn met the dragon. The dragon looked fierce. The dragon flew away because the unicorn scared him.

The next day, the unicorn went home. When she went home, she was very happy.

Ollie Askew (6)
Northside Primary School, Northside

The Shy Crab And A Scary Shark

Once upon a time, in a faraway sea, there was a magical speedboat. Down in the dark blue sea, there was a sparkling red crab with his friends. All of a sudden, a scary shark came and ate all of the fish for his breakfast. A sparkling mermaid called Jasmine scared the shark away and said, "Don't come back again." The mermaid and the king were very excited because the shark would never come back. The mermaid and the king swam to the top of the bay and pushed the boat away.

Emelia-Niamh Davies (6)
Plasmarl Primary School, Plasmarl

The Cheeky Crab

Once upon a time, there was a little paddling boat sailing across the bay.

Under the sea, a cheeky crab was trying to play with the fish. Suddenly, a big, creepy shark came along and the crab hid in its shell. The glittery mermaid came and climbed onto the shark's back and frightened the shark away. The mermaid and the king were happy and the crab and the seahorse started dancing. The mermaid and the king swam to the boat to stay safe.

Lilly Rose Samuel (6)
Plasmarl Primary School, Plasmarl

The Little Mermaid

Once upon a time, there was an empty boat floating on the salty sea. At the bottom of the sea, there was a pinchy crab and he was looking for his friends. Suddenly, a scary shark came and frightened the crab away. Then along came a sparkly mermaid and she said, "Shoo!" to the shark.

Next, the crab moved out of his shell and said thank you to the amazing mermaid. Everyone swam up to the floating boat and had an amazing party.

Lucy New (6)
Plasmarl Primary School, Plasmarl

The Big Bad Shark

Once upon a time, there was a gigantic boat far away in the blue sea.

Down in the dark blue sea, there was a very naughty crab who was pinching the fish. Suddenly, the crab hid in his shell because a scary shark came to eat him! Then a blue mermaid came too close to the huge shark and he got trapped. Everyone had a party and it was amazing. The mermaids swam to the top of the sea and had a picnic in the boat.

Jayden Thomas (6)

Plasmarl Primary School, Plasmarl

The Swimming Mermaid

Once upon a time, there was a medium-sized boat sailing on the crashing waves.
In the deep blue sea, a red crab was eating all the soft seaweed. Then a fat shark came and was about to eat the crunchy crab! A mermaid came along and shouted at the nasty shark, "Stop!" Everyone had an amazing party and they even had a water cake! They all swam up to carry on the party at the top of the sea.

Charlotte Lynch (6)
Plasmarl Primary School, Plasmarl

A Beautiful, Fun Sea

There was once an abandoned boat sailing out to sea. A really cheeky crab named Yammy was gardening his crab garden in the undersea town but a bully shark stole some plants from the crab's garden. The king's daughter scared the really mean bully shark away. Everyone was so happy they had a dance party.

In the end, the crab made a house on the boat, the boat sunk to the bottom of the sea.

Iestyn Thomas (6)

Plasmarl Primary School, Plasmarl

The Craziest Story In The World

Once upon a time, there was a little boat slowly sailing out to sea. Under the salty sea, a red, cheeky crab was taking all the food. Suddenly, a gigantic shark with sharp teeth frightened everyone, except the seaweed. Then an amazing mermaid came who said to the naughty shark, "Get away!" The shark never ever came back again and everyone was very happy. The very naughty shark was defeated!

Max Murphy Jenkins (6)
Plasmarl Primary School, Plasmarl

The Singing Mermaid

Once upon a time, there was a boat on the salty water. A crab was telling the fish, "We need to get to the boat for a party!" Suddenly, a mean shark came to eat the shiny, red crab and the fish. A shiny mermaid heard someone yelling for help. The mermaid said to the shark, "Shoo!"
Everyone said, "Hooray!"
In the end, the mermaid had a picnic on the boat.

Rylee Watts (6)
Plasmarl Primary School, Plasmarl

Under The Water

Once upon a time, there was an empty boat floating on the blue sea. In the salty water, there was a pinching crab pinching the fish. Suddenly, a shark with big teeth scared the fish away. Along came the mermaid named Cinderella and she scared the shark away with her singing voice. Everyone was happy because she'd scared the shark away. Cinderella and the king were very excited.

Daniel Chrapek (6)
Plasmarl Primary School, Plasmarl

The Nice, Sparkly Mermaid

Once upon a time, there was a boat on the salty sea. At the bottom of the sea, a crab was trying to eat fish for her dinner. Suddenly, a scary shark tried to eat the crab, then a brave mermaid came and said, "Shoo," to the shark. The mermaid and the king danced because the mermaid saved the day.
In the end, the mermaid and the king jumped onto the boat and went out.

Tiana Clayton (6)
Plasmarl Primary School, Plasmarl

The Cheeky Crab

Once upon a time, there was a boat sailing on the shiny, blue sea. There was a red crab trying to find his friends in the sea. The shark came looking for the crab. The mermaid said, "Stop!" The mermaid said, "I'm happy because the shark has gone." The mermaid was very happy!

T J Smith (6)
Plasmarl Primary School, Plasmarl

Natalya's Under The Sea Story

Once upon a time, there was a boat sailing on the sea. The red crab was trying to eat the fish. Suddenly, a blue shark came and ate the crab. The mermaid slapped the shark. The pretty mermaid had a party with her king dad.
In the end, they sailed across the sea.

Natalya Antonia Dare (6)
Plasmarl Primary School, Plasmarl

The Glitter Mermaid

Once upon a time, there was a boat on the really deep sea. A cheeky crab was pinching all of the food! Then a scary shark scared away the hermit crab. A glittery mermaid scared away the scary shark and the mermaid had a party. The mermaid had a picnic on the boat.

Tyarna-Leigh Davies (6)
Plasmarl Primary School, Plasmarl

Into The Secret Woods

One stormy night, there was a loud bang. Jack and Josh woke with a fright. They both looked out of their bedroom window. Out of their window, the brothers could see the magical woods. The boys were feeling brave and went to investigate the mysterious woods.

In the woods, they saw eyes looking at them. The boys moved in closer to see the big green eyes. It was a killer snake! The snake spoke to the boys, "Well, well, two tasty boys for my dinner!"

Jack and Josh ran away as fast as they could. Luckily, they came across their old pal Leo the lion. They told Leo about the snake wanting to eat them so Leo protected the brothers and chased the snake away. The boys were happy never to see the wicked snake ever again. Leo, Jack and Josh played all day.

Alexis Hamilton-Simmons (7)

Prendergast Community Primary School, Prendergast

Magical Animals

Once upon a time, there was a girl named Polly. She went for a walk in the woods with her dad and dog, Dougal. Dougal saw a squirrel and chased after it. Polly dropped the lead and ran after Dougal. Her dad was talking on his phone so he didn't notice that Polly and Dougal had gone missing.

The squirrel, Dougal and Polly ran into a clearing in the woods and saw a lion, rabbit, fox, deer and a woodpecker all sat in a circle. Polly couldn't believe it. The animals were talking and she could understand them! The squirrel, Dougal and Polly joined in with them. The lion asked, "Polly, what are you doing in the woods?"

"I got lost chasing Dougal," said Polly.

The fox said, "Do you want us to help find your dad?"

"Yes please," said Polly. "How come I can understand you?" asked Polly.

The deer said, "It's because you're in the magical woods. Do you want to go now?"

"Yes please as my dad will be worried, but I will miss you."

The animals put their magic together and then Polly and Dougal were back with Polly's dad again in the blink of an eye.

Holly Helga Jane Thomas (6)

Prendergast Community Primary School, Prendergast

Connor's Jungle Story

I was walking to my house, then I got lost in a big, scary jungle. The bats were staring at me with their mysterious eyes. I met a snake, the snake was brown and he blended in with the tree branches. The snake said to me, "If you follow the path, you will see a python and it will try to eat you."
I ran fast and saw another path. I then met a lion who ran to ask me something. He said, "Follow me." So I ran with the lion really fast, the air shook past me. The lion ran to an apple and banana tree and we ate them all. I felt great after eating them and had the strength to walk home.
I saw my house. I felt happy to be home. I was sad to say goodbye to the lion because it was nice meeting him but I said I would see him soon.

Connor Halsall (6)
Prendergast Community Primary School, Prendergast

The Hermit Crab And The Mermaids

One day, a boat was floating in the middle of the sea but when the birds started to loop-the-loop in the sky, the boat started to sink to the bottom of the sea.

In the coral reef, all of the creatures were really frightened except the hermit crab. Then a big shark came, it was huge! The hermit crab quickly got into its shell but the shark could smell the crab. "Oh no!" cried the crab. Luckily, a mermaid came to the rescue and scared the shark away. Her dad saw everything. "Thank you," said the crab. "If it wasn't for you, I would have been a shark's lunch." Everybody cheered, "Hooray! Hooray!" Then the mermaids brought the boat up to the surface. "Woohoo, the mermaids did it!"

Kenuli Himadya Wickramaarchchi (6)

Prendergast Community Primary School, Prendergast

The Boys' Adventure

Once upon a time, there were two boys called Ben and Mike. Their adventure was a walk in the woods. The boys got lost in the spooky woods. The boys saw a snake on the way to the spooky woods. The boys were scared when they saw the snake. They screamed for help. They got really scared! Someone came to their rescue. It was a big, furry lion! He had big, furry ears that heard the boys' shout. The lion was called Pan. The lion scared the snake away. Ben and Mike were safe! The boys said thank you for saving them.

The lion showed the two boys the way home. They followed Pan until it was dark. The lion was hungry so the boys asked him to stay for dinner. They all had fun and promised to be best friends forever.

Megan Roos Conings (6)

Prendergast Community Primary School, Prendergast

Charlotte's Magical Story

Once upon a time, there was a princess called Olivia who lived with her pet unicorn and her mum, the Queen.

One day, a dragon came by. He came looking for the unicorn because he wanted to eat it. He breathed fire and a tree fell down onto the castle roof. He kept breathing fire to get the unicorn so he could eat it. Olivia was very nervous and frightened so she hid under her bed. The pet unicorn wasn't frightened and bravely went outside. But instead of frightening the dragon, it gave some food to the dragon. The dragon wasn't hungry anymore so became nice. The dragon flew back home and he wasn't nasty anymore because he ate fruit.

Olivia and her pet unicorn lived happily ever after.

Charlotte Ella Isaac (6)

Prendergast Community Primary School, Prendergast

The Little Rowing Boat

On a cool summer's day, the little boat decided to set out for an adventure by himself to see how big the ocean was. The fish and Crabby waved as he sailed by. Everyone was very happy to see the little rowing boat.

Then a dark shadow came along and everyone hid. It was Biff the shark, the meanest, baddest shark around! He scared Crabby back into his shell.

Then King Neptune and Lilly the mermaid said, "Biff, stop being such a bully."

Biff said "Sorry" and swam off.

Lilly, Neptune and Crabby danced under the sea after Biff the bully had gone. They all waved good luck to the rowing boat and off he sailed into the sunset.

Jacob Smith (6)
Prendergast Community Primary School, Prendergast

Shark Bait

I always wanted to see a shark. When I went on holiday, we went out on a boat. Daddy asked the captain if I could go in the cage and see a shark. I put a diving suit on and got into the cage with Daddy. The cage went down into the water. The rope snapped and we went to the bottom! There was a great white shark the size of a boat swimming around us. The shark kept hitting the cage and it broke. We swam to an underwater cave to hide. Three dolphins arrived and saw us. They chased the shark away. Daddy and me swam out of the cave and up to the boat.
I'd like to go in a cage and see a shark again but I hope it's a stronger cage!

Lucas Cameron Hull (7)

Prendergast Community Primary School, Prendergast

The Lion And The Snake

One sunny afternoon, I was looking for flowers in the woods. When I looked up, I saw eyes staring at me through the trees. One of the animals approached. The animal looked very friendly. As the animal got closer, I recognised it was a snake but suddenly, the snake bit me on my arm! A lion came to save me. The lion bit the snake and the snake slithered away. I felt upset when the snake bit me but was surprised when the lion came out of the bushes. I made friends with the lion, then the lion took me home. I said bye to the lion and the lion said it back.

Oliver Harri Lowe (7)
Prendergast Community Primary School, Prendergast

Deep In The Jungle

There are lots of animals in the jungle, but what is it like in the jungle? I would like to find out.

There's a snake in the jungle, slithering through the trees and it's camouflaged because it's the same colour as the leaves. There's a python coming towards a lion. It's coming closer!

"Boo!" shouts the lion as he jumps out the bushes, he is excited. The lion is also friendly. The lion is running around the python in excitement! "Let's go home and have a barbecue," says the lion.

Sam Warneford (6)

Prendergast Community Primary School, Prendergast

Deep In The Jungle

There lived a lion and a snake. The snake tried to eat the lion, the lion was nice, the snake was bad. The snake slithered along a branch. He was sneaking up on prey, waiting for the right time to strike. He then hissed in the lion's face. The lion jumped and pounced at the snake and then the snake slithered away but the lion followed him. The lion ran around him playfully. They made friends, then the lion said, "Follow me so you can come for dinner with me. We are having cookies and milk and banana sauce!"

Mollie Mathias (6)
Prendergast Community Primary School, Prendergast

Scary Jungle

Welcome to Scary Jungle. The jungle was very scary because it had lots of scary animals. One of the animals in the jungle was a snake called Sam. Sam liked the jungle and wanted the jungle all to himself. Sam was angry when he saw another animal in the jungle. A lion lived in the jungle too, his name was Liam. Liam didn't like the angry snake. Liam decided to run away from the jungle to find a better place to live.

Liam found a great house to live in in a quiet, friendly area. Liam is so much happier now.

Lucas Tate (6)
Prendergast Community Primary School, Prendergast

Splash

I went on a boat fishing. I caught a fish. The fish was blue. The fish pulled me off the boat! I saw lots of seaweed and fish. Out of the seaweed came a shark. He had big, sharp teeth and he wanted to eat me for his dinner. Suddenly, a mermaid came out of the seaweed and flipped him on his nose with her tail. The shark zoomed away, his nose stung.

The mermaid and her dad shouted, "Hooray!" They did the floss. They helped me get to my boat. They waved goodbye and I went back home.

Josh Oxley (6)
Prendergast Community Primary School, Prendergast

Harry The Lion's Big Adventure

Hi, my name is Harry the lion. It's dark in the forest tonight so I want to go on an adventure. I think I can hear a snake moving in the trees. Now I can see him. I hope he is a nice snake! Argh, he has seen me! Oh silly me, it's just Sniper the snake! I think he wants to play hide-and-seek. I hide in the grass, where he won't see me.

It's nearly morning now, I have had fun in the forest. I am going to go home for some nice, tasty breakfast.

Zac Morris (6)
Prendergast Community Primary School, Prendergast

Shark Survival

Once upon a time, I was on my speedboat. I found an empty boat five metres from the shore. I went diving, looking for clues. Under the water, I saw some sea creatures. All the sea animals swam away from the shark. What could I do? the shark got scared and turned away because of the mermaids. All the sea creatures came back and lived happily with the mermaids. I said thank you to the mermaids and drove off on my speedboat.

Tomos William Blyth (5)
Prendergast Community Primary School, Prendergast

The Knight, The Fairy And The Big Dragon

In a tall tower, there was a fairy. She did a spell. It didn't go so well. The only reason - it made a dragon! The dragon breathed fire on the tower. The kingdom was in trouble! The dragon blew fire at some of the houses until a knight called Sir Knight of Bravens galloped up on his horse. He fought the dragon. The knight won and then he married the fairy and she wasn't allowed to do any more spells!

Charlie Dunthorne (6)

Prendergast Community Primary School, Prendergast

The Lost Rowing Boat

Once upon a time, there was a little rowing boat. It was just floating above some sea creatures having a party. There was a crab and a fish and a starfish. The seaweed was waving in the water. A nasty-looking shark was feeling hungry. It swam towards them. The king and a mermaid came to the rescue. They scared the shark away. They were all happy, they joined in with the party. They all waved goodbye.

Caitlin Jackson (7)
Prendergast Community Primary School, Prendergast

The Sea Adventure

We spotted a blue boat on the quiet sea but hiding underneath was Mr Crab, the fish family and a seahorse. Out jumped the big shark with his sharp teeth. "Oh no!" Then a beautiful mermaid came and the shark looked afraid.

Once the shark went, the mermaids had a sea party. They even woke up the little blue boat with all their singing and dancing!

Reuben Thomas (6)

Prendergast Community Primary School, Prendergast

Callum's Story

One day, I went fishing in a boat. It was a sunny day. There were fish in the sea. Then I saw a shark. Along came some mermaids that sent the shark away. Everyone was happy.

Callum Ceri Davies (6)
Prendergast Community Primary School, Prendergast

Millie's Magical Story

One day, there was a castle in Rainbow Forest. There was a princess in the castle, she was the prettiest princess in the world.

One day, there was a dragon that came. He was a very, very frightening dragon. Everyone ran away when they saw him. The dragon nearly blew down the house but luckily, it was made of brick and the windows were made of plastic. The unicorn and the dragon fought. Luckily, the unicorn won and everything was safe. The dragon was so scared, he said, "Mum, I need you so much!"

"What is the matter?"

"I let myself down."

The unicorn lived happily ever after.

Millie Webster (6)

Quainton CE Primary School, Quainton

The Princess And The Prince

Once upon a time, in Rainbow Woods, there was a lovely princess called Victoria. She was asleep. Princess Victoria was the daughter of the queen and King Charming, they were good to her. Princess Victoria was ever so kind.

Princess Victoria was going to a ball but she had nothing to go in, then she went in a car. A witch was near, she wanted to kidnap the princess! When the princess was about to go home, she ripped the princess' gloves off her and looked around. The witch went to a dungeon and the princess went to sleep.

Scarlett Ashton (6)
Quainton CE Primary School, Quainton

Harriet's First Story

Once upon a time, in the jungle, there was a tiger called Jack. Jack was a cub, cubs get into a lot of danger! He had a friend. He waited for the lion that he called Jake and they got into trouble. They went to the crocodile lake. Every time, they nearly got into trouble but this time, the crocodile leader knew that Jack and Jake were cubs. Jake said, "Come on!" They jumped into the lake. The crocodiles ate the fish.

"I won't eat you," the crocodiles said. The mum found the cubs because it was bedtime.

Harriet Aplin (6)

Quainton CE Primary School, Quainton

Dinosaur World

Once upon a time, there was a time machine. A man walked across it and then it went *pow!* When he opened his eyes, he was in Dinosaur Land. He walked to a lava pool and when he got there, a T-rex went for him! The man said, "Help!" Suddenly, a diplodocus saved him. The T-rex felt angry and walked off and had a drink to calm down.

In the meantime, the diplodocus and the man made friends. The diplodocus helped him survive. He gave him food and shelter and they lived happily ever after.

Harry William Espiner (6)
Quainton CE Primary School, Quainton

The Heart Of The Wolf

Once upon a time, there was a wolf and one day, he went into the woods. A knight chased the wolf. The wolf ran and ran but he ran into a hole and he was scared of the noises. A workman found him and took him to the princess. The princess said, "Make him a bed and food and water and put him in the shiniest cage ever." The workmen were building the biggest castle to live in in the world for the princess and the wolf.

By the time it was built, they were tired and left out of breath and sweating!

Jake Kehoe (6)
Quainton CE Primary School, Quainton

Harley's First Story

Once upon a time, there were two unicorns. They were looking for a rainbow. One of them had to go up to the Pegasus and talk to it to find the rainbow. The Pegasus led the way. The unicorn ran as fast as she could. They would finally get to see it! She told her sister and she screamed really loud. The Pegasus and the unicorn had a little chat. "Be careful, the rainbow is very powerful!"
She finally got to see it. It was beautiful. She screamed again. She ran to get her sister, they both ran.

Harley Sayell (6)
Quainton CE Primary School, Quainton

Back In Time

Forc had a back-in-time machine. He used it and he went to a dinosaur world. Forc found a dinosaur. They could be friends! The dinosaur was a nice dinosaur. The dinosaur was chasing Forc for a laugh. Forc was tired so the dinosaur picked him up and he slept on him. He was sleeping on his tail. Forc was sad so he went into the machine. He went home. Suddenly, the dinosaur came with him!

Dilan Marudamuthu (6)
Quainton CE Primary School, Quainton

Ava's Magical Story

Once, there was a beautiful castle with a princess inside. She saw a dragon coming closer and closer and closer to the castle!
When he got there, he fired the castle down! Then a unicorn came and fought the dragon and the dragon got upset so he flew away. The princess made a new home. The unicorn asked if she could live with her. She said yes and they lived happily ever after.

Ava Patricia Read (6)
Quainton CE Primary School, Quainton

The Girl Lost In The Forest

One day, a girl went to the forest and she saw a fox. She got scratched! Then she saw a snake and it was really nice. He let the girl have a sweet. And then a horrible snake came and it didn't give her a sweet. Then she saw a lion and he left a sweet at her door. She saw the nice lion again, it was really nice. Then she saw a lion with a gem, he was nice too!

Alice Carlisle (6)

Quainton CE Primary School, Quainton

Lucas' First Story

A long way out in the deep blue sea, there lived a shark but it wasn't an ordinary shark, it was a rainbow shark and the rainbow shark had sharp, dirty teeth. First, a blue squid came and said, "Please can I have one little, sharp tooth?"
The rainbow shark said, "No, who do you think you are?" Next, the rainbow shark went to go to a stingray for advice.
The stingray said, "I can't help you with that but if you go to the coral reef, you will find a wise seahorse." The rainbow shark went to see the wise seahorse.
The wise seahorse said, "I have been waiting for you, this is my advice. Give one of your sharp teeth to the fish."
Finally, the rainbow shark went and the blue squid came along again.
"Don't be angry, I just want a little, sharp tooth."
The rainbow shark said, "Hmmm, I will give you one little tooth." Then the rainbow shark had lots of friends.

Lucas Thompson (7)
Rogerstone Primary School, Rogerstone

Alfie's First Story

A long way out in the deep blue sea, there lived a dolphin. Not an ordinary dolphin but the most beautiful dolphin in the entire ocean.

One day, a little, blue sea lion came and said, "Please can you teach me some of your tricks?" The rainbow dolphin said, "No, who do you think you are?" Then the little, blue sea lion swam away and told all his friends what had happened, then no one had anything to do with the rainbow dolphin. When he swam past, they swam away. Then the rainbow dolphin went to see the seal. "I can't help but if you go to the coral reef and go to the deepest cave, you will find the wise shark." So the rainbow dolphin went to the wise shark. The wise shark said, "I have been waiting for you. Show the sea lion some tricks."

The sea lion and the rainbow dolphin became friends.

Alfie Downs (6)

Rogerstone Primary School, Rogerstone

Lauren's First Story

A long way out in the deep blue sea, there lived an octopus but the most beautiful octopus in the ocean with rainbow tentacles.

One day, a pink jellyfish came and said, "Please can I have a tentacle?"

The rainbow octopus said, "No, who do you think you are? Get away from me." The pink jellyfish went away.

The octopus found a stingray. "I can't help you but if you go through the coral reef, you will find the wise turtle, he can help you," said the stingray. So the rainbow octopus swam a long way to see the turtle.

At last, the rainbow octopus found the wise turtle, the turtle said, "The waves have told me your story. This is my advice, give a tentacle to the pink jellyfish."

So the rainbow octopus went and gave a tentacle to the pink jellyfish and they became friends.

Lauren
Rogerstone Primary School, Rogerstone

Emily's First Story

A long way out in the deep blue sea, there lived a beautiful rainbow dolphin, but not any dolphin, it had beautiful scales.

One day, a little, blue seahorse followed him and asked, "Please may I have one of your scales?" The rainbow dolphin said, "Who do you think you are?" The rainbow dolphin went to see his friend, the red jellyfish. "Why doesn't anybody like me?" said the rainbow dolphin.

The red jellyfish said, "I cannot help, you need to go and see the wise squid." So the rainbow dolphin set off to find the wise squid.

Once he found the squid, he said, "The waves have told me your story. Share your scales with the little, blue seahorse." So he went back to see the little, blue seahorse and he shared his scales and they were all happy.

Emily Faulds (6)
Rogerstone Primary School, Rogerstone

William's First Story

A long way out in the deep blue sea, there lived a mermaid. Not just an ordinary mermaid, the most popular mermaid in the entire ocean.

One day, a little, orange starfish came along and said, "Can I have one of your shiny scales? You have so many."

"You think I'm going to give you one of my shiny scales? Who do you think you are?" Then the starfish told all of his friends.

The mermaid went to see the sea lion for advice. "Why does everybody like me?"

"I can't answer that. Go to the wise octopus, he will help you."

So the rainbow mermaid went to see the wise octopus. "Why does everybody like me?"

"Share your scales with the sea creatures." So the mermaid gave away her scales, then she felt fantastic!

William Jude Woodley (6)
Rogerstone Primary School, Rogerstone

Dewi's First Story

A long way out in the deep blue sea, there lived a rainbow shark, not just any ordinary shark but the most beautiful shark! The rainbow shark had six colourful teeth.

One day, a little, black stingray came and he asked for the orange tooth, the shark said no, then the stingray swam away. Next, the rainbow shark saw the wise dolphin. "I can't help you, go and see the crab, he can help you."

The shark went to see the crab. "I can help you. Give one tooth to all the other fish." Then there was a little touch of a fin. The little stingray. The shark gave a tooth to the stingray. Suddenly, the shark was surrounded by other fish. The rainbow shark went left and right and then suddenly, he had one tooth left. He felt happy.

Dewi Munn (6)
Rogerstone Primary School, Rogerstone

Olivia's First Story

A long way out in the deep blue sea, there lived a rainbow dolphin. Not just any ordinary dolphin but the most beautiful in the entire ocean.

One day, a little, purple seahorse came and said, "Please may you show me your tricks?"

"No," said the rainbow dolphin. The rainbow dolphin went to see the grey shark.

"I can't help but if you go and see the orange squid, she can help you," said the grey shark.

"Sorry to bother you," said the rainbow shark.

"Show the purple seahorse your tricks!" So the rainbow dolphin enjoyed showing his tricks, jumping over waves and swimming in zigzags. Finally, they became best friends forever.

Olivia (7)
Rogerstone Primary School, Rogerstone

Pietro's First Story

A long way in the deep blue sea, there lived a rainbow crab but not just an ordinary crab, the most beautiful crab in the sea. Everyone wanted his shell.

One day, a blue shark said, "Can I have your shell?"

"You want my shell?"

From that day on, nobody wanted to play with the rainbow crab. He asked a stingray, "Can I come help you?"

The wise stingray said, "I've been waiting for you. Find other shells and give them to the fish." He found his shells and gave one to the shark.

"Thank you," said the shark. The crab decided to give the other shells to the other fish. He was happy because he had a lot of friends.

Pietro Christopher Kaye (6)
Rogerstone Primary School, Rogerstone

Ffion's First Story

A long way out in the deep blue sea, there lived a rainbow whale.

One day, a little eel fish swam by and he asked, "Can I please have a bit of your skin?"

He said, "No, who do you think you are? Get away from me." Shocked, the little eel fish swam away and then the rainbow whale went to see the crab. The crab said, "I can't help you, go and see the stingray." He went there.

The stingray said, "Go and find some gems." He did.

Finally, he found some gems and he went to find the little eel fish. He gave the gems to him and there were best friends and they were both happy.

Ffion Rose Newman (6)
Rogerstone Primary School, Rogerstone

The Rainbow Lobster

Once upon a time, there was a lobster. Not just an ordinary lobster but the most beautiful lobster. His friends called him Rainbow Lobster and he lived in a pile of rocks.

One day, he was playing with his friend, the dolphin with the wavy tail. They played hopscotch and when he was going to jump to the number seven, he jumped the wrong way and bumped his claw on a rock! He had to go to Doctor Stingray. He put a bandage on it and went back in six weeks. The doctor took off the bandage. When it was taken off, they had a celebration and all of his other friends came too.

Lydia Porter (6)
Rogerstone Primary School, Rogerstone

Brooke's First Story

A long way out in the deep, dark sea, there lived a rainbow dolphin.

One day, a little turtle came along. The little turtle asked for the rainbow fin. The rainbow dolphin said no so the little turtle went. The rainbow dolphin was sad so he told his troubles to the starfish. "Maybe you can go to the shark, maybe he can help you." So he went to the shark.

"Go find some shells." So he went to find some shells.

After, the little turtle came over. He took some shells out of his pocket and gave them to the turtle. They were happy.

Brooke Barnes (7)
Rogerstone Primary School, Rogerstone

The Rainbow Dolphin

Once upon a time, there lived a dolphin but not just any ordinary dolphin, one of the most beautiful dolphins in the entire ocean. He lived in the coral reef.

One day, he found a new, sparkly starfish friend and they both went to a dark, spooky cave and the rainbowfish got lost in the dark, dark cave, he was scared!

Finally, the sparkly starfish found him and they found a trail of purple, sparkly shelves and it led them home. Everybody was really, really scared about where they had gone so they had a super nice party!

Katy Cooper (6)
Rogerstone Primary School, Rogerstone

The Rainbow Swordfish

One day, there was a swordfish but not an ordinary swordfish, the most beautiful swordfish! One day, the rainbow swordfish saw some plastic and he picked it up and swam home, but he got lost in a cave! He went to the wise octopus in the cave. The octopus said, "Follow the torch and the rope." So the swordfish followed the torch and the rope back out of the cave and when he came out, he saw his friend, the seahorse.

When he got back, he put the plastic in the bin and went to get some more.

Dylan Hugh Matthews (6)
Rogerstone Primary School, Rogerstone

Ben's First Story

A long way out in the deep blue sea, there lived a shark. Not just any shark, it was the most beautiful shark in the world.

One day, a sea turtle came along. He asked for a colourful tooth. The rainbow shark said, "No, who do you think you are?" The rainbow shark then said to the wise starfish, "Why doesn't everybody like me?"

"Because you don't share your teeth. If you share your teeth you will discover how to be happy." He shared his teeth, then he was happy.

Benjamin Jacob Jones (6)
Rogerstone Primary School, Rogerstone

Rainbow Eel

Once upon a time, there was an eel, not just an ordinary eel, the most beautiful eel in the entire ocean. He lived in-between some dark rocks in the sea. He was playing tag.

One day, Starfish came to play but they got lost. Then they saw an octopus and he said, "Follow the shells, then you'll find your way home."

Starfish and the eel found the shells. Their friends were worried! As fast as a flash, the eel and the starfish were there. They said, "We are glad to be home."

Theo Austin Phillips (6)
Rogerstone Primary School, Rogerstone

Rylie-Faye's First Story

A long way out in the deep blue, there was a seahorse. Not just an ordinary seahorse, a rainbow seahorse! A shark said, "Can I have one of your shiny scales?"

"No," said the seahorse. "Who do you think you are?" He went to see the jellyfish.

"Go and see the starfish, she will give you some advice," she said.

"You have to share your shiny scales," said the starfish. The seahorse shared his scales with the shark. The seahorse was happy.

Rylie-Faye Harry-Young (6)

Rogerstone Primary School, Rogerstone

Rainbow Starfish

Once upon a time, there lived a rainbow starfish. Not just an ordinary starfish, the most beautiful starfish in the entire ocean. He lived by a deep, dark cave and he had a friend called Octopus.
One day, they went deep into the dark sea.
Octopus said, "I am scared." Then they met a wise eel.
"Follow the bubbles to get home," he said so they did and they got home again.
Rainbow Starfish said, "I am glad we are home again." Then they had a party.

Ella Manning (6)
Rogerstone Primary School, Rogerstone

Isla's First Story

A long way out in the deep blue sea lived a rainbow stingray.

One day, a blue dolphin said, "Can I have your shiny tail?"

"No," said the rainbow stingray, "go away!" The rainbow stingray poured his troubles to the turtle. "I can't help you. If you go to the coral reef, you will find the wise crab."

"Give a scale instead of your tail." He did what he was told. He offered his scale instead of his tail and went home.

Isla Mae Fox-Smith (6)
Rogerstone Primary School, Rogerstone

Rainbow Dolphin

Once upon a time, there lived a dolphin but not just an ordinary dolphin, the most beautiful dolphin in the entire ocean. His friends called him Rainbow Dolphin. Rainbow Dolphin's friend was Octopus and they played a game of hopscotch. Then they changed their minds and played a game of hide-and-seek. Octopus got lost and Octopus' tentacles got stuck, then the dolphin came to rescue Octopus and then Octopus was free. Octopus and Dolphin lived happily ever after.

Grace Davis (6)
Rogerstone Primary School, Rogerstone

Rainbow Octopus

Once upon a time, there lived a rainbow octopus, not just an ordinary octopus but the most beautiful octopus in the entire ocean. She lived in a dark, gloomy cave. Her friend was a seahorse.
One day, they played hide-and-seek, then the rainbow octopus got lost so she asked the starfish. The starfish said, "Follow the current and it will lead you home." So she did and she saw her friend and they celebrated and they played hopscotch.

Emilia Wendy Casagrande (6)
Rogerstone Primary School, Rogerstone

The Rainbow Octopus

Once upon a time, there was an octopus but not an ordinary octopus, the most beautiful octopus in the whole ocean. There was a coral reef. The octopus saw lots of fish. He met another friend and they played hide-and-seek, the rainbowfish was 'it'. The octopus hid in his cave and the starfish hid behind the rocks and the seaweed. The rainbowfish found the starfish. Then the starfish found the octopus. They went home.

Max Chambers (5)
Rogerstone Primary School, Rogerstone

Corey's First Story

A long way out in the deep blue sea, there lived a rainbow dolphin. An octopus said, "Can you show me some of your tricks?"

He said, "No." He went to see the turtle.

"I can't help you. Go and see the seal, he will help you."

When the octopus came back, he asked, "Will you show me your tricks?"

"Yes, I will," he said. They became friends.

Corey Jai Morris (6)
Rogerstone Primary School, Rogerstone

Rainbow Eel

Once, there was a beautiful eel, not just any ordinary eel but the most beautiful eel in the entire ocean. He lived in-between some dark grey rocks at the bottom of the sea. He met an octopus that was green with long tentacles. The octopus lived in a cave. The rainbow eel and the octopus played tag and they got lost! They found some shells to get them back home to the race and the cave, then they had a party.

Zachary Slade
Rogerstone Primary School, Rogerstone

The Rainbow Squid

Once upon a time, there lived a squid. Not just an ordinary squid, the most beautiful squid in the ocean. His friends were a seahorse and a starfish. One day, they decided to play hide-and-seek but the starfish got lost! They looked at the bottom of the sea. He was there. They played a game of tag. Jellyfish and Octopus asked if they could play. They said yes so they played together, happily ever after.

Poppy Marie Davies (6)
Rogerstone Primary School, Rogerstone

The Rainbow Lanternfish

Once upon a time, there was a lanternfish but not just an ordinary lanternfish but the most beautiful fish in the entire ocean. It was a rainbow lanternfish. He found new friends, they were a friendly shark and a starfish. They all played hide-and-seek and the lanternfish was it but the lanternfish found both of them! They all lived happily ever after.

Mackenzie Stone
Rogerstone Primary School, Rogerstone

Rainbow Swordfish

Once upon a time, there was a swordfish, not just an ordinary fish, it was a rainbow swordfish! He was with his friend, Lanternfish. They were playing tag but they got lost! But then they swam past an octopus and the octopus said, "I might know where your home is." But they didn't trust him. Then the waves took them back to the seaweed.

Shouvik Sengupta (6)

Rogerstone Primary School, Rogerstone

My Rainbow Crab

One day, a little, green crab had a friend who was a jellyfish and a light fish. The light fish put his light on. They started to go down. The little, green crab hid under a rock and the jellyfish hid in the seaweed. The light fish was putting his light on so he could see the fish, then they started to go up. Then they started to have a party!

Harvey Tayor (6)
Rogerstone Primary School, Rogerstone

Rainbow Octopus

Once upon a time, there lived a rainbow octopus, not just an ordinary octopus but the most beautiful octopus in the ocean.

One day, he was playing in the seaweed and then he got lost. He met a starfish. The starfish was shiny and pretty. The starfish said, "Follow the shells." So they followed the shells and he was home again.

Gracie Meyrick
Rogerstone Primary School, Rogerstone

The Rainbow Dolphin Story

Once upon a time, there was a dolphin who was a rainbow dolphin.

One day, she went out with her friends and they played hide-and-seek. She hid under a rock and she hurt herself. She told her mum and her mum put a plaster on it. They had to get to her house and then they helped everybody get ready for the party.

Freya Williams (6)

Rogerstone Primary School, Rogerstone

My Rainbow Seahorse

Once upon a time, there was a seahorse but not just an ordinary seahorse, his friends called him Rainbow Seahorse.

One day, he got lost but he found an octopus, then he remembered he left a trail of pebbles.

When he got back, his friends were waiting to welcome him back home into the seaweed.

Hazel May Read (5)

Rogerstone Primary School, Rogerstone

The Rainbow Seahorse

Once upon a time, there was a rainbow seahorse. One day, the rainbow seahorse went to play with his friends. They played hide-and-seek but then, the rainbow seahorse got lost but he had lots and lots of stories to tell them when he was back home with all of his friends!

Oliver Bowen (6)
Rogerstone Primary School, Rogerstone

The Rainbow Whale

Once upon a time, there was a rainbow whale. It was pink and golden and red. The whale was playing tag and then he got lost. He went to see the octopus and he swam there really fast.
He found his friends by the seaweed so they played tag again.

Freddie Hayes (6)
Rogerstone Primary School, Rogerstone

My Rainbow Unicorn Fish

Once upon a time, there was a beautiful fish called Rainbow Unicorn Fish. Her friend was a starfish. They played tag.
One day, they saw a lanternfish, he was afraid.
They swam away and then they became friends.

Maia-Tlws Blackler

Rogerstone Primary School, Rogerstone

The Kind Unicorn

Once upon a time, in a faraway land, there was a little kingdom named Unicorn Kingdom. There lived the nice queen of the unicorns named Lula. The kingdom was quite comfortable.

One day, the kingdom was approached by a dragon. Queen Lula was surprised and scared at the same time. She ordered all the guards to prepare for a battle and attacked the dragon. While the guards were busy preparing, the dragon suddenly roared in pain. The dragon cried for help but no one could understand him.

Finally, he breathed fire out his mouth as a sign of asking for help. "Help!" said the dragon. Soon enough, Lula understood what the dragon wanted to say.

She approached the dragon and asked, "What happened? May I help you?"

The dragon couldn't understand unicorn language so he only showed his injured hand.

He had a splinter! With Lula's magical healing powers, she carefully took out the splinter from the dragon's hand and the dragon had a sigh of relief. The dragon thanked Lula for her help and flew away. Lula felt so happy to help others.

Delisha Saabira Yasni
Sekolah Darma Bangsa School, Kedaton

Rex The T-Rex

I opened the magic book and it took me back in time on a dinosaur adventure. I used a time machine.

When I got there, I saw a diplodocus and a stegosaurus and they were eating some plants. I saw a T-rex. He looked scary but he was actually really nice and his name was Rex, the T-rex. He was just hunting. Next, I saw a nest. The nest had some eggs in it. "Who do these belong to?" I asked.

"They belong to me."

"Who is that?"

"The pterodactyl."

"Oh no, the volcano is erupting!"

"Come on, you can climb on top of me." *Phew!* The volcano stopped erupting.

"Sorry but I have to go home. The time machine changes colour when I have to go."

Thomas Steven Burden (6)
Sound Primary School, Lerwick

My Adventure To A Jungle

I opened a magic book and it took me on a jungle adventure.

The snake was very scary and hungry. I was scared of the snake. The snake was slithering up the tree. His name was Bobby. He was very scary. He had a long tongue. He had sharp teeth, his eyes were funny. A lion jumped out at the snake. He killed the snake!

The lion was friendly. Me and the lion played outside and had fun. The lion played in the park. Me and the friendly lion went home. The lion was sad when I had to go home.

Connor Burgess (6)
Sound Primary School, Lerwick

Magical

Once upon a time, I flew to a magic castle. Then there was a rainbow. When the rainbow went away, there was a dragon that could breathe fire! It was very fierce. The dragon was very hungry so it went to look for food. Then a beautiful unicorn came and it used its magical horn to make the dragon happy. The dragon flew away to find some friends.

Finally, he found some friends, then he fell in love with one and then the unicorn did.

Natalia Kerr Leggate (5)
Sound Primary School, Lerwick

My Trip To The Jungle

I opened the magic book and it took me on a jungle adventure. It was scary, there were spooky eyes everywhere in the jungle.

A snake was looking sad and it was stuck in the tree. It was going to fall down from the jungle tree! It was very, very scary, she was mad! A lion fell down into the jungly leaves. It was weird because it fell and it didn't have a scratch! The lion went back home and I went back home too.

Nina Hughson (5)
Sound Primary School, Lerwick

The Land Of Magical

Once upon a time, there was a magical land and there was a princess. The princess was very magical but one day, a dragon came to destroy the magical land! The dragon was very fiery! One day, a unicorn came to destroy the dragon and the unicorn was very beautiful. It scared the dragon away and the dragon flew back home. The unicorn went home too, outside the princess' house. They lived happily ever after.

Ella-Mae Gair (5)
Sound Primary School, Lerwick

My Under The Sea Adventure

I opened the magic book and I jumped into the sea. I was happy but the water was cold. I met a crab and his name was Snappy. He said hello. He was crazy! Then I saw a shark and it chased me and it tried to chase me away. Then I saw a mermaid and I saw the king. I saw a seahorse. We celebrated. Everybody was happy. The sea people said, "Bye, come back soon!" Then I got home in time for dinner.

Jacob Henderson (5)
Sound Primary School, Lerwick

My Adventure In The Jungle

I opened the magic book and it took me on a jungle adventure. Then I saw scary eyes, then I saw a snake. Was it a good or bad snake? I didn't know! It slithered out of a tree, then I found out it was a bad snake. It had its mouth open. Then a lion jumped out, he was happy. It was cute, it was yellow. He scared the snake away. We went for a walk, it was fun. Guess where I went with the lion? Home!

Daniel Anderson (6)
Sound Primary School, Lerwick

130

The Day I Went To See Dinosaurs

I opened the magic book and it took me on a dinosaur adventure. I saw a volcano erupting, there was lava. There were two dinosaurs. I saw a T-rex, he was scary! He was red, he ate the leaves. He was angry.

Next, the T-rex tried to get the eggs but the nest fell down. The pterodactyl came home, he was sad because the nest had fallen down.

We went home, it was an exciting adventure!

Lowrie Nicol (6)
Sound Primary School, Lerwick

My Adventure To The Jungle

I opened the magic book and it took me on a jungle adventure. I explored the jungle. I found a snake and he was fierce. He was on the trees, on a branch. It was freaky, I ran for my life! His hiss was scary and his teeth were sharp. Then a lion came and the snake saw the lion. The snake was cross. The lion ran to save the day. He ran out of the bushes and bit the snake. Then I went home.

Lewie Johnston (5)
Sound Primary School, Lerwick

Under The Sea

Once upon a time, I went rowing on my boat. Suddenly, a big wave came and I fell off my boat. Suddenly, a ship. "Watch out!" A shark was behind me.

"Grrr!" I ran for my life. Suddenly, *smack!* "Argh!" Then the shark swam for his life. Nobody saw the shark again. They had a party.

"Woohoo!" They all lived happily ever after.

Zena Roseanne Wiseman (6)
Sound Primary School, Lerwick

My First Under The Sea Adventure

I went to the sea for my adventure. I found a boat, then I saw a crab and I saw fish, it was black and white. There was seaweed.
"Oh no! There is a shark and it is scary!"
A mermaid scared the shark away. The king came and there was a seahorse. They had a party and so did the seahorse. The crab came to the party too! The mermaid said, "Bye-bye!"

Freya Byrne (5)
Sound Primary School, Lerwick

My Adventure Called Time Machine

I went on the time machine, it took me to the dinosaurs. I saw a diplodocus, he was eating leaves. A volcano was erupting! The diplodocus ran but he couldn't run fast. A T-rex popped out of the bushes, he was a bad T-rex. A pterodactyl laid eggs, they were in a tree. The pterodactyl flew away. The pterodactyl was looking for food. I went on the time machine to go back home.

Corren Williamson (5)
Sound Primary School, Lerwick

It Was Time To Go To The Jungle

I opened the magic book and it took me on a jungle adventure. I found lions and there were thirteen of them. I had their crown, they were going to chase me!

A snake was looking for his nest because he was bringing food. The snake was chasing me and he was poisonous! A lion sprung on me. The lion was hunting. The lion was looking for me, I hid in the log and I went home.

Cole Kay (5)
Sound Primary School, Lerwick

Under The Sea

One beautiful day, me and my friend found a boat. It was an orange boat and we fell out of the boat. Then we met a crab. The crab was called Chloe. Then a shark came to eat the fish! It was hungry. A mermaid and a merman came to scare the shark away, then I was hungry so I wanted to go home. After all, we were out at sea.

We got home, then we had fish and chips.

Magnus Leask (6)

Sound Primary School, Lerwick

When I Was In The Jungle

When I went to the jungle, I saw a snake. It was a friendly snake and it was red. It slithered away and I didn't see it again. But then I saw another scary snake, it had a long, red tongue and teeth. Suddenly, a lion jumped out. It ran towards the snake and pounced but it jumped so far that it landed right at the start of the jungle, where my house is!

Amie Coleman (6)
Sound Primary School, Lerwick

My Adventure

I opened the magic book. It was an adventure back to the dinosaurs.

The volcano was erupting, it was lava. The T-rex was popping out of the leaves. There was an egg in a nest in a tree and the tree was small. The egg was the pterodactyl's. The pterodactyl was flying in the sky.

Now I was back home, I could still see the time machine!

Theo Spence (6)

Sound Primary School, Lerwick

The Jungle Adventure

In my adventure book, there were cat eyes looking out of the trees. I met a friendly snake in the jungle. He was nice. The snake wasn't really friendly. He had a long tongue. Then there was a friendly lion. He was cute and he was looking out and hiding in the trees. The lion ran through the trees. I met him climbing on a rock on my way home.

Lily-May McLean (5)
Sound Primary School, Lerwick

My Adventure To A Jungle

I opened the book and it took me on a jungle adventure. I saw a snake and it was crawling on a stick. He told me his name was Sam. Sam was cross and he had sharp teeth. His tongue was red and long. A lion came with sharp claws that tore leaves. The lion brought me home and he ran faster and faster. I walked and ran as fast as I could!

Adam Spence (6)
Sound Primary School, Lerwick

Dinosaur Land

Once upon a time, a stand came but it was a magical stand.
Next, there was a place called Dinosaur Land and it had lots of dinosaurs. Then a T-rex came. It gave me a threat, I ran away as fast as I could. What happened next? There was a nasty dragon. When he got closer, I got him. Then the dragon took me home. I waved goodbye.

Luca Thomason (6)
Sound Primary School, Lerwick

The Story About A Space Adventure

I opened the magic book and it took me on a space adventure. It took me around the world but not in the world. An alien took me in his space saucer and it had lots of buttons and levers. The alien told me he was called Sam. He had three eyes.

He took me back home and I was back in time for tea. It was soup, it was yummy!

Leila Hall (6)

Sound Primary School, Lerwick

My Adventure To The Jungle

I opened the magic book and it took me on a jungle adventure. I met a snake and he was a red snake, he was scary and told me his name was Roman. He scared me a little. A lion started to roar and he scared the snake but he was friendly. The snake slithered away. The lion ran home. My home was a little bit away.

Darcey Henry (5)
Sound Primary School, Lerwick

My Undersea Adventure

I went underwater and I had an adventure. I met a crab and two fish. We played hide-and-seek.
I met an angry shark and his name was Sharky. He was going to attack the kingdom!
I met a king, he scared off the shark. We had a dance. The crab played hide-and-seek with us. We waved goodbye.

Leon Priestley (5)
Sound Primary School, Lerwick

My Trip Under The Sea

I sailed to the magic undersea world. I met a crazy crab. His name was Snappy. I saw a metal shark. I wasn't scared. His name was Snappy too! And I saw a king, he was sorting the shark out. He was using his trident. They had a party. They did some dance moves. They said goodbye and I went home.

Charlie More (5)
Sound Primary School, Lerwick

A Jungle Adventure

I saw spooky eyes in the trees and I hid in the bushes. I ran away and I met a snake. He was on the tree. I scared him. The snake was biting me and it was sore! A lion cut the snake in half with his claws, then the lion followed me to my home. We said goodbye and I had my dinner.

Oarryn Mann (5)
Sound Primary School, Lerwick

My Trip To The Bottom Of The Sea

I opened the book and it took me on an adventure. I met a crab. His name was Crabby and he was under the sea. The shark was a bad shark. The shark scared the king and was bad to the king so the mermaid saved the kingdom. The mermaid and the king said goodbye and I said it too.

Natas Engum (5)

Sound Primary School, Lerwick

My Story About A Jungle

I opened the magic book and it took me on a jungle adventure.

I saw a snake, he was a very happy snake. He was so long.

Then there was an angry snake, I was scared.

A lion came, he saved my life. I got a ride from the lion.

Me and the lion stood on a log.

Nathan Ross (5)
Sound Primary School, Lerwick

Dinosaur Land

I made a time machine and I went to Dinosaur Land.
There was a T-rex and I was scared. There were three little eggs and they were dinosaurs. There was a flying dinosaur.
I went back home in the machine.

Alfie Tozer (5)
Sound Primary School, Lerwick

My Undersea Adventure

I opened the magic book and it took me under the sea. I met a crab and he was happy. A shark came and had sharp teeth. The mermaid scared the shark away. The mermaid and the king had a party. I had to go home.

Alec Arthur (6)

Sound Primary School, Lerwick

Space Adventure

Once upon a time, a spaceship went to space.
The rocket fell out of space.
A flying saucer was coming, a bad alien was coming!
The alien picked up the spaceship. The spaceship went on a path.

Daniel Henry (6)
Sound Primary School, Lerwick

Dinosaur Land

One day, I found a time machine.

I saw a dinosaur and there was a volcano! There was a T-rex who was protecting the eggs and the little pterodactyl.

I used the machine to get back to the future.

Nebble March (5)

Sound Primary School, Lerwick

Under The Sea

One day, I saw a red boat. I fell off my red boat, then I saw a friendly crab. Then I saw a fierce shark and then the mermaid came. The mermaid lived happily ever after. They waved at me on the boat.

Bella Smith (5)
Sound Primary School, Lerwick

The Unicorn Saves The Day

Once upon a time, there was a beautiful, pink, candyfloss castle. Everybody kept coming to the castle and started to eat the pink candyfloss castle. The king didn't like it at all! Then suddenly, a dragon came to the castle and had a look around, then he saw the pink, fluffy candyfloss. "Oh no!"

When he saw the pink candyfloss, he started to blow fire onto the pink, fluffy candyfloss. The king was worried about his castle.

When the dragon wasn't looking, a unicorn came up behind the dragon and then the dragon touched the unicorn and *poof!* The dragon flew away deep into the sky. The unicorn was very proud of herself, then the unicorn was so happy, some sparkles came.

A few nights later, the unicorn was walking through the woods, she found a little house hiding. No one lived in it so she decided to live in it.

Lily Jennifer Trainor (7)
St Mary's Primary School, Portaferry

The Unicorn Defeats The Dragon

Once upon a time, there was a pretty castle on a hill, then a dragon appeared outside the castle. He had a scaly body and he breathed fire. A unicorn came and defeated the dragon. Then the dragon breathed fire, it got angrier and angrier, the dragon was so angry he breathed the most fire he could!

One minute after, the fire stopped. The dragon touched the unicorn. The dragon got scared, really scared! Soon, the dragon's foot got hotter and hotter. He said, "Oh no, my foot is so hot." The dragon flew away. The unicorn was very happy so she ran home. "I am very happy because I scared the dragon away!"

"I am happy I have found my home. I am going to see if there are any children nearby then I will have some friends." They lived happily ever after.

Cahlie Boyd (7)
St Mary's Primary School, Portaferry

The Mermaid And The Shark

Once upon a time, there was a beautiful boat and the boat was pink, blue and purple. The boat was far, far out from home. No one could see it. Under the boat were a lot of colourful fish. Some were big, some were small, some were in-between big and small. Most of the big animals were fierce and scary. Suddenly, a big shark came and scared all of the animals away, but not one creature, Rosetta the princess mermaid! She was trying to defeat the shark and her dad came along and helped her defeat the shark.

At last, they had defeated the shark and had a big party. They sang songs and danced with sea creatures until the day was over.

Later on, they went up to the surface and found the boat.

They hopped onto the boat and sailed away to another castle to live in forever.

Eva-Marie Curran (7)

St Mary's Primary School, Portaferry

Space

Once upon a time, there was a rocket. It was broken, it was hard to fix.

After they finally fixed it, they tried it, then it broke again!

Next, they tried it again. They were tired, it flew very fast! It flew past Earth and Mars and all the other planets. Then they saw some stars, the stars were yellow. They saw the moon, the moon was white. It was dark.

In the end, they saw a green alien. The green alien looked friendly. It was friendly, it loved people coming. The green alien took the rocket away, now they could get back to their houses. The alien took the rocket to their house.

They finally got home, it took a long time to get home, their rocket had broken but the alien fixed it. They went to bed.

Francis Keating (7)
St Mary's Primary School, Portaferry

Jungle Story

Once upon a time, there was a forest that had a jungle. There was a snake and a lion with creepy eyes and the snake was so, so scared. The snake went onto a tree and some animals fell off the tree. The lion roared and the snake fell off the tree. The tree nearly fell down!

The snake started to be scary. The lion said, "I will be climbing my tree too." They used to play together at the park and other people would come and play if they didn't want to.

"Are we friends again?" The lion ran off and fell on the nettles. He ran into a tree and the branches. He was so shocked. The lion went back home to bed and went to sleep, he was tired.

Ellie McGrattan (7)
St Mary's Primary School, Portaferry

The Under The Water Adventure

Once upon a time, in a faraway land, a boat was out far at sea. It might have been shipwrecked because there was no one in the boat.
Meanwhile, under the sea there were different kinds of fish, there were small fish, big fish, thin fish, fat fish! The seaweed was all different colours. "Argh!" screamed the animals and swam off to hide when a shark appeared out of nowhere. It had a creepy smile. A mermaid saw him and it didn't work. Her dad made him leave that part of the ocean.
After that, they were happy for the rest of their lives and they lived happily ever after.

Caitlin Ritchie (7)
St Mary's Primary School, Portaferry

The Nice Alien

Once upon a time, there was a spaceman. He wanted to travel around Earth in a rocket but what happened next? There was a crack, a bit came off the rocket. "Come and help me!" There was a flash and a fizz. A UFO appeared. He went as fast as he could go to save the rocket but the spaceman didn't know what was happening.

An alien came out of the UFO but the alien got back in the UFO and started it up and then lifted the rocket. He brought it back to Earth to look for his home. They looked over the mountains. They found the house and then they had a party for the alien.

Jude Coleman (7)
St Mary's Primary School, Portaferry

The Crash

Once upon a time, a rocket was in space zooming across the stars. Suddenly, the rocket's leg fell off! It crashed on Mars. Lying on the hard, sandy floor, time flew by just sitting there.

Suddenly, a UFO appeared. The stars were getting closer and closer and then something was peeking out. A happy, smiley alien was sitting there waving right in front of him. "Right, stop doing that now please." And then the alien and the UFO slowly pulled up the rocket into the UFO.

They brought the rocket home but the alien forgot to bring the leg back, silly alien!

Joel McKenna (7)
St Mary's Primary School, Portaferry

Castle

Once upon a time, there was a castle with a rainbow on top. There was a tree and a path. A dinosaur came to the castle. The dinosaur had scales. The dinosaur saw the castle, he attacked the castle but he couldn't beat it. Then he could do it, he fired at it and the building burnt. The roof came off, the unicorn was still on it. "Everyone, the roof is off!" The unicorn used magic, it made the dinosaur good again. The dinosaur flew away.
It was night so the unicorn went to sleep because she found a house.

Scarlett Trainor (7)

St Mary's Primary School, Portaferry

The Dragon And The Unicorn

Once upon a time, there was a castle. It was pink and beautiful. A rainbow formed behind it and a unicorn lived in it. The unicorn was bright pink. Just then, a dragon came. He was the worst dragon in the kingdom. He set fire to anything that came into sight. He set fire to the castle and a knight couldn't stop him. He was the strongest dragon in the world! Then a unicorn came and said, "Stop! What are you doing here?" The unicorn scared the dragon. They all lived happily ever after.

Caitlin Hall (7)
St Mary's Primary School, Portaferry

In The Wild Jungle

Once, there was a very creepy forest in the dark lands of the jungle. There was a snake on a tree branch looking for food.

After, the snake got frustrated because he didn't find any food. Then a lion heard all the racket in the jungle and peeked in the grass. When he saw the lion, he ran as fast as he could. The lion escaped the jungle.

Evan Morgan (7)

St Mary's Primary School, Portaferry

Castle

Once upon a time, there was a castle with a rainbow on top of it. A dinosaur came to the castle. The dinosaur had scales. The dinosaur got soaked by the rain. The big dinosaur got very angry. A lovely unicorn came along and dried him. He became very happy! The dinosaur flew home, leaving the unicorn.

Lily-May Elizabeth Marshall (7)
St Mary's Primary School, Portaferry

Space Adventure

The rocket was broken, it had crashed into a planet. The ship fell onto the planet and it was broken. There was a UFO. "Hi, my name is Aron, I will help you, don't worry!" The alien helped me and we fixed the ship.
"Yay, I am home! Yay! Yay!"

Kenzie McCluskey (7)
St Mary's Primary School, Portaferry

The Cross Dragon

Once upon a time, there lived a unicorn called Evie. She lived in a castle.

One day, she went out for a lovely walk in the woods. She went with a basket so she could pick flowers. Evie loved the woods.

One day, a dragon came to Unicorn Land and he was a green dragon with red scales and a hot-red mouth with sharp teeth. That day, he came to Evie's house when she was away. He walked up to the castle and had a bad idea. He would set the castle on fire and that was just what he did! With one big blow, he set the castle on fire.

On the way back home, Evie met the dragon. The dragon froze and took Evie's hand. The dragon suddenly started to say, "Evie dear, I set your house on fire." When Evie heard this, she burst into floods of tears.

After a while, Evie said, "Mr Dragon, I am very cross." With that, the dragon flew away. Evie was sad because her house had got burnt away.

After walking the whole night, she found a cottage and she walked up the lane. Evie lived happily ever after.

Rose Tallon (7)
St Patrick's Primary School, Aughagallon

The Girl And The Dragon

Once, there was a girl without a mum or dad. Her dad got old and her mum died in a car crash. Her name was Lucy. Lucy had to walk everywhere. One day, Lucy went for a walk. On the way, she met a dragon. He was mean! He captured Lucy and kept her as a slave. The dragon was very, very lazy! Poor Lucy had to do all of the work.

An enemy came one day, the dragon had a big fight. Lucy tried to escape but slipped in a magic puddle and it changed her into a unicorn! Lucy had very loud steps because of her hooves. The dragon heard her and they had a big fight. Lucy scared the dragon away.

After that, Lucy went home and lived happily ever after.

Katrina Brankin (7)

St Patrick's Primary School, Aughagallon

My Dinosaur

I made a time machine to go to the future to Dinosaur Land. In the next moment, the time machine had stopped. "We must be here!" Then I saw a dinosaur. I saw a dinosaur attack another dinosaur! Then I turned around and saw a dinosaur right behind me. I had to make a run for it.
The next morning, I got up and I saw a nest up in a tree. I went to pick it up and I saw a crack in the egg. It started to get very dark so I went to bed. The next morning, I said goodbye to the dinosaurs I'd met, it was time to go home.

Ronan Hughes (7)
St Patrick's Primary School, Aughagallon

Magic Land

Once upon a time, there was a land called Magic Land. Magic Land was very bright and colourful. One day, a dragon came to Magic Land, he was not happy. Then the dragon breathed fire beside the castle. The unicorn wondered what was wrong. The dragon came over to the unicorn and said, "Will you marry me?" The unicorn refused. The dragon flew away in anger, never to be seen again. The unicorn decided to go and visit her friend the fairy and tell her the good news, that the dragon had left Magic Land!

Anna Corey (7)
St Patrick's Primary School, Aughagallon

The Snake And The Lion

Once upon a time, there was a forest. It looked scary and creepy but Eva had to go through the forest to get to her friend's house on the other side. Eva spotted a snake in the tree, she wondered if he was a friendly snake but then he snarled at Eva and she jumped and shouted, "Help!" Then a big, friendly lion appeared. He scared the snake. He chased away the angry snake. Eva was very, very thankful! The lion helped Eva through the forest to her friend's house. They became best friends forever.

Eva Anna-Marie Lavery (6)
St Patrick's Primary School, Aughagallon

Space

Once upon a time, there was a rocket that zoomed out of this world.
It went back to Earth and crashed beside a house.
The alien saw it and the alien said, "Hello."
The alien lifted the rocket up, then took the rocket back to outer space.

Jay Mulholland (7)

St Patrick's Primary School, Aughagallon

The Snake Tale

Once upon a time, there was a big snake in the forest and there was also a snake in the woods. Suddenly, a big snake scared a lion. The lion was frightened so he hid behind the bushes. He ran away from the snake. Then the snake and the lion became best friends.

Charlie Nelson (7)
St Patrick's Primary School, Aughagallon

George's Under The Sea Story

George was going on an adventure. He set off out to sea in a rowing boat. George dived into the sea. There he met Herman the hermit crab and his fishy friends. Mr Shiny Shark tried to eat Herman the hermit crab so he hid in his shell. George saw what was happening and went to get help. He found the king and queen of the sea people. The sea people were happy because the shark had been captured by the king and queen. The king and queen waved to George.

George Edward Heaps (5)

Stanwix Primary School, Carlisle

A Cumbrian Adventure

In Maryport, I took a rowing boat out to sea and went diving to see my friends, Mr Crab and Mr Fish. Mr Shark was in a very grumpy mood and he was being nasty to everyone! Arla the mermaid told Mr Shark off, so Mr Shark said sorry and swam away quickly. Arla and her dad, King Titan, were so happy. We had a victory dance! Then it was time to leave. Everyone came to say goodbye.

Sophia Willow Rawlings-Brown (5)
Stanwix Primary School, Carlisle

Lily And The Desert Island

Lily wanted to find a desert island. She went on a boat and she came to the desert island. She saw lots of fish. Then she saw the treasure! She opened the treasure chest. She grabbed the gold, then Lily went back to the boat. Lily sailed back to Lulu and they had a party and the other teddies came to the party.

Mathilde Zayer (5)
Stanwix Primary School, Carlisle

Under The Sea

Once upon a time, there was a little fishing boat on the sea. Mr Crab lived in the sea with his fishy friends. Mr Shark was really bad, he ate fish. Mr Shark was scared of the mermaids. The mermaids were dancing. The merking turned bad and chased the mermaids.

Annabel Fraser (5)
Stanwix Primary School, Carlisle

My Trip To Bangladesh

This summer, I went on an amazing adventure with my special boat. I met many creatures, crabs and fish and then a naughty shark attacked me but a beautiful mermaid and her daddy saved me. Their names were Aida and King Daddy. We became best friends.

Arman Kalam (4)

Stanwix Primary School, Carlisle

The Little Mermaid

Once upon a time, a man went to see a little boat. He saw a crab on the sand. A little fish was hiding from the shark. The mermaid was putting her hand up. They were happy. The mermaid was waving at the boat.

Harriet Ryding (5)

Stanwix Primary School, Carlisle

Little Red Fish

Once upon a time, a sailor fell into the sea. He met a little, red fish. A big shark came along. A mermaid chased it away. Then they had a big party. They all lived happily ever after.

Austin Barry (4)

Stanwix Primary School, Carlisle

Water Heroes

I was in a boat. I saw fish and crabs. Along came a shark. "Boo!" The mermaid scared the shark. The mermaid saved the day!

Thomas Van Lierop (4)
Stanwix Primary School, Carlisle

Angharad's Dinosaur Story

There was a little boy, his name was Paul. He had a computer. He came to Dino World. Paul shook and shivered when he saw dinosaurs. He walked closer. There was a volcano erupting. Paul and the dinosaurs went to the trees. There, in the bushes, was a T-rex, he secretly walked to see the nest of eggs. He stole the eggs and ran away! Everybody ran, then the pterodactyl caught the T-rex and fought him and poked him with his beak. Then Paul said that he had to go home and got home. His mum took him into the café for dinner.

Angharad Bowen (6)
Stepaside CP School, Kilgetty

Jacqueline's Dinosaur Story

In the attic, I found an old time machine. I sat on the magic chair. It took me back in time to Dinosaur World. There were lots of kind dinosaurs. The volcano was erupting in Dinosaur World. There was a T-rex, the T-rex saw three eggs and stole one egg! The baby eggs hatched out of the eggs, they played with each other. The nest was about to fall down! The pterodactyl came back when she saw the nest on the floor. I went to find the three eggs. I found the babies. I sat on the chair, I got home. I went into the house.

Jacqueline Dunfee (7)
Stepaside CP School, Kilgetty

Back In Time

Once upon a time, there was an explorer. He sat on the chair and went back to Dinosaur World. When the explorer got to Dinosaur World, he found some dinosaurs and a volcano erupting. A tyrannosaurus rex stole the eggs! There were three eggs in the nest.

When the pterodactyl got back, the eggs were gone. The explorer found the eggs high in the tree. The explorer got the eggs, he put the eggs in his back and went back to the nest. The explorer went back to the chair.

Liam Lee
Stepaside CP School, Kilgetty

Dinosaur Adventure

Once upon a time, there was a time machine. Tom sat in the time machine. It took Tom to Dinosaur Land! The brontosaurus took Tom to the kind T-rex. The kind T-rex helped Tom and the brontosaurus to get out of the way so Tom and the brontosaurus wouldn't get hurt. The pterodactyl eggs hatched. The pterodactyl was flying home to see if they had hatched. It was so happy! There was the time machine to go back home, Tom was so excited.

Lisa Stevens (6)
Stepaside CP School, Kilgetty

World Of Dinosaurs

Me and Morgan were playing outside. Morgan saw a rusty, old chair. We both sat on it. We were in a dinosaur lab and we saw 500 dinosaurs! The big eggs belonged to the T-rex. A dinosaur was flying high in the sky. Then we went home.

Connor James Jones (7)
Stepaside CP School, Kilgetty

The Magic Princess

Once upon a time, there was a princess and a prince who lived together. The princess' name was Zara and the prince was called Ricky. Ricky and Zara looked out of the window and they saw a dragon. Zara screamed. The dragon's name was Fire. He burnt the rainbow and the tree down and he almost burnt the castle down but he stopped because Poppy the unicorn came. The dragon was evil. The unicorn huffed and huffed and blew the dragon away from the princess but he was coming back quick! "Poppy the unicorn, save us!"

"I'm back, you can't stop me," the dragon said. Fire backed away. Poppy the unicorn followed him and blew him away, the fight was over.

"Stay back, or else!" Fire the dragon flew away fast and Zara and Ricky came out of the castle.

"Thank you, Poppy," Zara said to the unicorn. "Will you live with us?"

"Yes!"

"Hooray! Let's go to the castle."

"Goodnight!" And they lived happily ever after.

Ella Wyn Bird (7)
Ysgol Y Graig, Lon Talwrn

Magical Creatures

It was one sunny morning, there was a beautiful princess and a queen and one handsome prince and king. They had a magical pet unicorn named Glitter.

The next day, a dragon appeared named Snow. He was called Snow because he was white. He was a nasty dragon, he had sharp teeth. The prince's name was Sam, the king's name was Archie, the princess was called Abi and the queen was called Holly. Some fire came out of the dragon's mouth. The unicorn got scared at first but then she wasn't. "This is really magical," said the king. The dragon and the unicorn could talk!

The unicorn scared the dragon away but first, Glitter told Snow, "You can't blow fire on my owners' beautiful castle!"

"You can't tell me what to do," said Snow.

"Good old Glitter," said Abi, Holly, Sam and Archie. The unicorn went for a walk, she found a little cottage and lots of magical unicorns and they had a party.

Ella Wyn Jones (6)
Ysgol Y Graig, Lon Talwrn

189

Billy's In The Jungle

One stormy night, on top of a big mountain, there was a forest, a dark, dark forest and creepy eyes, angry eyes, the bushes were scary. A big, long snake lived in the forest. Jason was his name. "I am lonely," said Jason. "What is that noise? I am afraid." Jason saw a bush moving. He got into battle mode. He had red eyes and his eyes grew. Jason shouted, "Whoever is behind the bush, show your face!" Jason went to find food.

A lion showed up. "I am Billy, I am strong. I think there is a snake around here. I am going to try to get a six-pack by running. I want a red and yellow snake for dinner!"

Here was Jason. "Let's fight!"

"Okay," said Billy. "Come on Jason! I am going to throw you!" said Billy. "Bye Jason," said Billy. "Ha ha! I am going home," said Billy.

Adam Pumfrey (7)
Ysgol Y Graig, Lon Talwrn

The Bad Shark

One rainy day, there was a little man named Tom. There was a shark that tipped the boat! Tom dived and swam as fast as he could. "Hi," said the crab. "Hello," said Tom.

"My name is Maya."

"Are you my friend?" said Tom.

"Yes," said Maya. Joe the shark came. Maya was scared. "Wow, Joe is fast."

"Maya, you're scared," said Joe, "I'm a rusher."

"Stop!" said Ella.

"What?" said Joe.

"You're stealing!"

"Stealing what?" said Joe.

"Stealing money," said Ella.

King Luke was happy and Queen Ella was happy. They were in love.

They liked everyone in the sea world but not the shark. The boat was safe in the sea because the shark was gone.

Bobby Parry (7)

Ysgol Y Graig, Lon Talwrn

The Unicorn And Dragon's Adventure

One sunny day, there was Queen Glitter, King Glitter, Princess Glitter and Baby Glitter in a ginormous castle. Near the castle, there was a dragon and a unicorn.

The princess looked through the window and there was a nasty dragon and she shouted, "Argh!" The dragon got angry and fire came out of his mouth. Now everybody was screaming. "Argh! Go away!" said the princess and the queen and the king. Suddenly, a unicorn came. The dragon and the unicorn were fighting.

The king said, "Come on Unicorn, you can do it!" The unicorn scared the dragon away. He flew away.

He shouted, "Argh! You are a scary, good unicorn." The unicorn went for a walk and a dragon came and told the unicorn to go this way. "Okay," said the unicorn. She lived happily ever after.

Lowri Evans (7)
Ysgol Y Graig, Lon Talwrn

The Fighting Adventure

In the dark, dark forest, there were big, spooky, scary eyes on the scary trees. There were hundreds of monsters on the trees.

In the forest, there was a snake moving on a branch in a tree, trying to find the big, skinny, strong, furry lion to fight him for dinner. Killer the snake found Smasher. They started to fight. Smasher did a backflip, kicked him in his face and Killer bit his belly but Smasher scratched Killer. Smasher won the fight, he was celebrating because he could eat him for dinner. Smasher was happy all the time with his friends. Smasher was running to meet his friends in the trees. Smasher was so excited to tell them he'd won the fight against the snake.

It was late. Smasher said, "I better go home now." So he was on his way home to his cosy bed in his house.

Gruffudd Huw Redvers Jones (7)

Ysgol Y Graig, Lon Talwrn

Jerry And Potter's Adventure

One night, there was a time machine that landed on the Earth. A man sat on the time machine and turned into a dinosaur. There were two dinosaurs that never hurt anyone. The dinosaurs' names were Jerry and Potter. They never stopped playing races and sleeping.

The T-rex was named Iolo. He ran at his eggs before the pterodactyl stole them. The T-rex killed the pterodactyl and ate him! The T-rex didn't leave the eggs. The eggs were hatching. The babies were happy, they were never angry. The name of the pterodactyl was Killer, he liked to steal eggs from other dinosaurs.

A man stole the time machine. The man turned into a dinosaur! The man who was a dinosaur turned into a man once more. Nobody found the time machine ever again. Every dinosaur was sad because the time machine was special.

Iolo Williams (6)
Ysgol Y Graig, Lon Talwrn

Rainbow's Magical Adventure

One sunny morning, there was a magical unicorn who lived in a palace by a tree and a rainbow, she lived by herself.

The next day, a nasty dragon came to the beautiful palace. The dragon blew fire onto the beautiful castle. "Argh!" shouted the unicorn. When the castle went down, the rainbow went invisible. The unicorn and the dragon became friends.

The dragon said, "What's your name?"

"My name is Maya," said Maya. "What's your name?"

"My name is Devi," said Devi. Then the dragon went back home and the unicorn went to build a new house. The unicorn went home to her new house to go and have food and to go to sleep.

Lexi Parry (7)

Ysgol Y Graig, Lon Talwrn

Adam The Diver And The Mermaids

One hot, hot morning, there was a boat in the middle of the sea. No one was on the boat because the boy was a diver.

There was a crab called Juyi, she was friendly. So were the fish. There was a white and orange fish. There was a nasty shark, her name was Caryl. She ate every kind of fish. She ate coral too. Caryl had sharp teeth.

Ariel's pet seahorse told Ariel, "Ariel! Ariel! There is a shark!" King Tryton poked the shark. They had a party, everyone came, Shelly, Juyi the crab, King Tryton and Ariel. They saw the diver, Adam. Ariel liked Adam. Ariel hugged Adam. They helped the diver and waved goodbye.

Ffion Haf Griffith (7)
Ysgol Y Graig, Lon Talwrn

Magical Unicorns

One really hot, hot day, I saw the unicorns. The unicorns were nice unicorns. I saw the magic unicorns. The unicorns didn't like Adam the dragon. Adam went to the unicorns. The unicorns were nasty to Adam and Adam was nasty. The unicorns were scary, they went to the castle. Everyone said to Adam, "Blah, blah, blah!" Adam said back to everyone, "Blah, blah, blah!" Adam flew away from the unicorns. The unicorns were happy because Adam flew away.
"We are happy," said the unicorns. They went back to the castle. The unicorns had a party.

Maya Golaski (7)
Ysgol Y Graig, Lon Talwrn

The Magical World Of Unicorns And Dragons

One sunny day, there was a castle with a king and queen. The castle was colourful and beautiful. Out of nowhere came a dragon, an evil dragon that tried to destroy the castle. The dragon tried to burn down the castle but the castle was indestructible. "Ha, ha, ha!" laughed the king and queen.

A unicorn named Ffion was magical. She fought the dragon named Maya. The dragon flew away because the unicorn scared her away. She felt like a hero! The unicorn went home but the magic made the day go to night. She lived happily ever after.

Cadi Lois Parry (7)
Ysgol Y Graig, Lon Talwrn

A Dinosaur's Big Fight

One day, there was a time machine. The time machine was fixed in a shop.

On a hot, hot day, there was Owen the dinosaur and a big, fat dinosaur. The two dinosaurs were friends.

One day, a T-rex attacked a nest of eggs. Nasty dinosaur! The pterodactyl stopped him from getting the eggs. The pterodactyl tried to take the eggs but the T-rex stopped the pterodactyl. The pterodactyl tried to find the T-rex for a fight in the forest. He found the T-rex and they had a big fight. The T-rex won. The time machine was fixed!

Owain Rhys Jones (6)

Ysgol Y Graig, Lon Talwrn

The Dinosaur Who Was Afraid

One sunny day, there was a time machine outside. Jeff went in the time machine to the dinosaur land. Suddenly, Jeff saw two dinosaurs in a field. The dinosaurs were eating grass. There was a T-rex who was shouting because he was angry. The dinosaur eggs were hatching. There was a squeaking noise. The pterodactyl flew to look for food in the forest. The time machine transported to a house. The people came out to try and move it.

George Henry Junior Takyi (7)
Ysgol Y Graig, Lon Talwrn

Efa's Under The Sea Story

Once, there was a green boat in the water. Under the water, there was a yellow and black fish that swam and a crab. The shark was being nasty to the fish and the crab. There was a pretty mermaid. The mermaid was trying to catch the shark. The shark swam away, scared of the mermaid. The mermaid was happy. The mermaid and the merman waved goodbye.

Efa (7)

Ysgol Y Graig, Lon Talwrn

The Storyboards

Here are the fun storyboards
children could choose from...

Jungle

Magical

Under the Sea

Space

Dinosaur

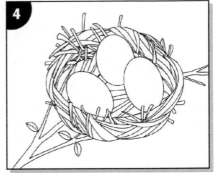

First published in Great Britain in 2018 by:

Young Writers
Remus House
Coltsfoot Drive
Peterborough
PE2 9BF
Telephone: 01733 890066
Website: www.youngwriters.co.uk

Young Writers Information

We hope you have enjoyed reading this book and that you will continue to in the coming years.

If you're a young writer who enjoys reading and creative writing, or the parent of an enthusiastic poet or story writer, do visit our website **www.youngwriters.co.uk**. Here you will find free competitions, workshops and games, as well as recommended reads, a poetry glossary and our blog.

If you would like to order further copies of this book, or any of our other titles give us a call or visit **www.youngwriters.co.uk**.

Young Writers
Remus House
Coltsfoot Drive
Peterborough
PE2 9BF

(01733) 890066
info@youngwriters.co.uk